Sharon struggled desperately with her bonds, but it was no good. He had tied them up all too tightly. And the gag was making it difficult for her to breathe again. What was she going to do? He would kill her. The salty tears coursed down her cheeks, and she wept until they would come no more. The panic surged and surged again until she could hardly breathe. If only someone would come . . .

Also by Anthony Masters

All the Fun of the Fair
(*Starling Point 1*)

Cat Burglars
(*Starling Point 2*)

African Queen
(*Starling Point 4*)

Badger

Streetwise

Dream Palace

JF 4698990

Siege

Anthony Masters

Teens · Mandarin

To my beloved son
Mark – whose quiet perception
and understanding never fails to amaze me

First published in Great Britain 1990
by Teens
an imprint of Mandarin Paperbacks
Michelin House, 81 Fulham Road, London SW3 6RB

Mandarin is an imprint of the Octopus Publishing Group

Copyright © Anthony Masters 1990

A CIP catalogue record for this title
is available from the British Library

ISBN 0 7497 0068 8

Printed in Great Britain
by Cox & Wyman Ltd, Reading

One

The day-room of the Victoria Hospital smelt of stale food. It was getting up to another morning of this that made Terry decide he was definitely going to do a bunk. He wanted to go home and explain everything to his parents. When he had done this, he was sure they would understand how Tessa died. He had been away for such a long time now and he really missed them. The only person he would miss here would be Janata, but he was leaving the hospital anyway. Janata was the only male nurse that he liked. The rest were either surly or stupid or downright brutal. He had been here too long anyway, and it was high time that he made a break. He was sure that Dad and Mum would take him back. They *had* to.

The milky coffee was slopped into the day-room at ten, and with it came Janata. He was tall and slim, part Asian and part something else that Terry could not make out. He came and sat down on the arm of the chair that Terry was sitting in.

'Are you going to play in the match?'

Terry shook his head. 'Can't be bothered,' he said, picking up a comic. At sixteen years old, Terry was big and very strong. He had been in this particular psychiatric hospital for a couple of years, ever since his dad had said he drowned his sister.

Terry had been in and out of hospital since he was twelve, when he had badly beaten up a boy who had bullied him at school. He just hadn't been able to stop hitting him somehow. With his clear, innocent face and long fair hair, Terry looked peaceful enough, but when he lost his temper he lost all control of himself and quite often had to be restrained by the nurses. But Terry had never attacked Janata. He liked him too much for that.

'You're a good footballer. Why not give it a swing?' Janata's voice was soft and warm and never threatening, even when he was trying to persuade Terry to do something. Janata felt it was important for Terry to get involved as much as possible; otherwise he sat in a chair all day and lived in his own private fantasy world.

'No,' replied Terry. 'Don't fancy it somehow.' His eyes were on the door. There were no locked doors. He could just walk out any time. The only question was when?

'We've got Janata a flat,' said Imran.

It was a summer Saturday morning at Starling Point and Imran and Sharon were helping to set up the August barbecue that was held every year in the central square. In the past the fair had often been there too, but recently they had taken to coming in September instead, so everyone wanted to make the barbecue really special, particularly for the old people who never got out and the kids who didn't have enough to do. The summer had been a really hot one. 'Just like the old days,' as old Mrs Willard had said to her deaf grandson Jonty. Jonty was with them now, helping to drag across one of the big barbecues. He could hear if you spoke really clearly and could lip-read well, and Sharon and Imran had grown used to him being part of their conversation in this slightly different way. But when Janata's name was mentioned Sharon frowned, for she was afraid.

Terry decided that the best time to make a break was after lunch. There was an atmosphere of torpor in the ward then; most of the patients slept while the nurses dozed. More importantly, the ever-watchful Janata was off duty. So Terry waited until he had his lunch of imitation curry followed by semolina, and then slipped out of the room, down the corridor and into the grounds. The only problem would be the gate-keeper's lodge, for Terry knew that he was on a section, which meant that he was not allowed outside the hospital grounds. The gate-keeper had a list of sectioned patients and he also took care to know everyone by sight. But Terry wasn't worried. He simply walked deeper into the grounds and eventually came to the woods that surrounded the hospital. It was not far from Starling Point here – probably a couple of hours' walk – and he was looking forward to the surprise that he was going to give his parents. They would really welcome him back when they saw him. He had lost weight too, for the only activity he took any pleasure in was exercising in the gym. He was really fit now and was sure they would be pleased about that too.

The hospital had been built as a series of separate low buildings and set in carefully laid-out grounds. To climb over the fence and into the woods was no problem at all, and soon Terry was walking down a sunlit path through the trees. He strolled along, perfectly happy. It was such a relief to get out of hospital. The long hot summer had made conditions in there really horrible.

As Terry ambled through the glades he pretended that he was with Tessa. She was two years younger than him and they had always played together as children; now he imagined they were playing together again. He saw her running in the woods and he began to run too, leaping in the air and jumping over brushwood and streams. He felt free and wild and wonderful.

'Is he coming to live here?'

'Dad wrote to the council and they gave him one of those emergency flats in B block.'

'Great,' said Jonty. He had met Janata at Imran's house a few months ago and liked him a lot.

Janata was a distant cousin of the Dapors, and although Jonty knew he was ill, he didn't know what disease he had. No one seemed to talk about it much. What he did know was that it upset Sharon a lot and that she was somehow afraid of Janata's illness. Several times she had quarrelled with Imran about it. Jonty also knew that she was ashamed about the arguments, but it was her fear that started them.

8

Now Jonty could sense there was trouble brewing between them again and he was sad because he was very fond of them both. Imran was rigid with tension as he arranged chairs round the barbecue, and Sharon was standing still, looking very worried.

'But will he be able to *live* on his own?' she was asking.

'Why not?' asked Imran irritably.

'Can he look after himself?'

'He's not an idiot.'

'I didn't say he was.'

'He'll be fine. He needs a rest and Dad's going to give him a light job in the supermarket. Just until he gets a bit less tired. All he has to do is to make sure he doesn't catch a cold or anything.'

'Wouldn't he be better off going home? Where his mum can look after him?' she asked hesitantly.

'You *know* he doesn't get on with his father. That's why he doesn't want to bother his mum.' Imran's voice was impatient and Jonty guessed they had been through all this before.

'Maybe she would like to be bothered.'

'She wouldn't.'

'Will you be going in there a lot?' Sharon finally brought out the question she had been so desperate to ask, and Jonty really felt for her. Imran's irritation increased.

'What do you mean?'

'I just mean – will you be going in there a lot?' Her voice quavered slightly and Jonty winced. Imran and Sharon had been going out together for a year now and they had surmounted so many of the problems they had originally faced. Although Mr and Mrs Dapor were strict Muslims they had accepted the relationship and welcomed Sharon into their home. It was only the Newbys, Sharon's narrow-minded parents, who disapproved and made life so difficult for her with their continuous prejudiced nagging. But despite all they had been through, Jonty knew that ever since Janata had turned up, Imran and Sharon had been on the edge of quarrelling.

'Of course I'll be going in there. He's not just a relative, he's a friend. Janata needs looking after and I shall do it, and so will my parents.' He ended on a note of challenging finality.

'What happens if he cuts himself?' said Sharon, provoked by his anger.

'What?'

'And his blood gets on you,' she finished in a rush, knowing that she was antagonising him even more.

'Are you crazy?'

'It's possible.'

'The trouble is that you're prejudiced against him. Just like your parents are prejudiced against me.'

'No.'

'You are. But you won't admit it.'

'I'm not. I'm sorry for him, that's all.'

'He doesn't need your sorrow – or your patronage,' Imran said with disgust.

'I'm not sorry in *that* way and I'm *not* patronising him.'

Jonty knew they were shouting now. He could hear them very clearly, too clearly, and tell from the way their lips were moving. Big, angry, shouting lips.

'You *are*.'

'Imran, I'm just worried, that's all.'

'Then don't be.' He suddenly turned away. 'I'm going down the shop to get some charcoal.'

'I'll come with you.'

'Don't bother. I'd rather be on my own.'

He walked away without a backward glance, and when Sharon turned to Jonty he could see that there were tears in her eyes.

'I've blown it now,' she said aloud, but almost to herself. 'I've really blown it.'

'He thinks you're against Janata,' said Jonty.

'I'm not,' she said. 'I'm afraid, that's all. Just afraid.'

Terry was sad when he left the protection of the woods. Tessa disappeared directly he came on to the streets. He looked at his watch. It was after three and getting even hotter. He was sweating, the pavement was boiling beneath his feet and he could see tar melting on the roads. But despite all this Terry still kept his spirits up at the thought of the welcome his parents would give him when he reached home. He began to jog, and suddenly his feet were as light as they had been in the woodland.

When Janata came back on duty at half-past three, he found that Terry had gone and no one had yet noticed. Cursing the laziness of the other staff, he went to the phone and called the police. They were very reassuring and thanked him for his call and told him that they would wait for Terry at his parents' house and yes – they did realise he was dangerous. They would know what to do.

'Please be gentle,' said Janata. They said they would, but he didn't believe them.

'You've got a long face, girl.'

Saturday teatime was usually dominated by the television in the Newby household and this one was no exception. Sharon's brother Mick was slumped on the sofa, to all intents and purposes asleep. She got on much better with him these days, and although he had been in trouble with the police last year, he now had a regular job at Mr Dapor's supermarket and was handling it well. He also had a regular girl-friend: Gallica, the African girl who had broken up with her boyfriend, Leroy, because he worked on a fairground ride and never saw anything of her.

Mrs Newby was reading the paper. It was only Mr Newby who had a roving eye for the emotional temperature of the family and who had developed the irritating habit of making personal comments with one eye on the television and the other on some luckless victim.

'A long face, girl,' he repeated.

'I'm fine,' said Sharon bleakly.

'Not been arguing with that Imran, then?' Mr Newby's voice had a triumphant note. Sharon had always been determined that he would never know what happened between her and Imran, but he had sensed that there had been something wrong recently and was anxious to make as much capital out of it as possible.

'No,' said Sharon briefly, trying to forestall any further conversation. But her father was persistent, patently trying to get her mother to join him in the calculated attack.

'You're looking so down in the mouth.' He was a specialist in clichés.

'Must be something wrong with my mouth, then,' she joked.

'You're listless,' he pronounced.

Sharon looked at her brother Mick, lying flat out on the sofa and now gently snoring. If she was listless, he must be dead. Her mother glanced up sharply and Sharon could see the pleasure in her father's eyes. He had got her going at last. How she hated him. One day Sharon would have the money to leave home and that would be that. She was sixteen now and in her last year of school. He'd better watch out, she thought. When she finally walked out she certainly wasn't coming back.

'You had a row with Imran, then?' her mother asked, and for a moment Sharon fancied that her father almost grinned in delight. But when she stared at him accusingly his mouth was like a rat trap of disapproval. 'No need to look at your father like that, my girl,' continued her mother, getting into her stride. 'Not after all he does for this family.'

That was pathetic, thought Sharon, for she was usually moaning at him fit to burst. She closed her eyes and waited for the droning accusations to flow over her. But instead they hurt her like tiny little darts.

'And open your eyes when I'm talking to you,' continued Mrs Newby.

Terry reached Starling Point after five. The heat was less intense and as he crossed the square he watched the preparations for the barbecue in pleasant anticipation. It looked as if it was going to be a lot of fun. Maybe Dad and Mum would take him. He sauntered across the square, savouring the moment when he would knock on the door and they would rush out and greet him with open arms. Then Terry had an idea. Theirs was a ground-floor flat just a few hundred metres from the square. It would be fun to peek in at the window and see what they were doing – see how they were coping without him. Terry grinned in delight. He had always loved surprises and now he was giving them one. It would be great fun to see their eyes light up at his sudden arrival. They had not been to see him at the hospital recently, but he guessed they had been busy. They were successful people, his parents. His dad was quite young and was the manager of the local sports shop and went down the squash club in the evenings. And his mum had a real passion for ballroom dancing. She had another bloke for a dancing partner, but Terry knew that that was only because Dad had two left feet. Now that Tessa had gone away, Terry was their only child and he looked forward to being a comfort to them in their old age, as one of the nurses had told him.

As he walked towards the flat, Terry returned to one of his happiest fantasies. His parents were old and crippled and confined to wheelchairs and he looked after them. They were dependent on him for everything and he would often wheel them round Starling Point. At first this had been tricky with single wheelchairs, but now he had invented a sort of double pram-like carriage for them both. He wheeled them out like babies, tucking in their blankets as he went. It was a good daydream and one he often dreamt, but now Terry was nearing the flat his thoughts returned to the happy surprise that he was going to give them. Sometimes they had shouted at him, particularly after what had happened to Tessa, but he knew that was all a misunderstanding.

'How do you feel?'

'Not so good. Just tired.'

Imran had met Janata at the flat in Starling Point's B block. Janata had picked up the key the previous day and had finally found the time to come and have a look round his new home. At the moment he had a tiny flat in the hospital, but it was poky and small and dismal, and now that he had given in his notice he would have to leave it at the end of the week anyway. He looked round the scruffy emergency accommodation and frowned. It didn't look much better.

'It's been a bad day. Chap called Terry Bonnington did a bunk.'

'Who is he?'

'Right nutter. Nice bloke, though. He did for his sister.'

'What do you mean?'

'Drowned her a couple of years ago.'

'Is he dangerous?'

'Only if he's in one of his rages.'

'Any idea where he could be?'

'Well, he could have come back here. His parents live somewhere on this estate.'

'That's nice.'

'Anyway the police have got it all in hand. And if he does go back to his mum and dad they'll nick him.'

'But he could be wandering about – ' said Imran. Janata seemed to be making light of a very alarming situation.

'I don't think he'll go far. Imran – '

'Yes?'

'It's very good of you and your family to help me like this.'

'We want to.'

'I know you do. I don't feel patronised or anything. Ever since I knew I was HIV positive I've been expecting people to patronise me, but I know you're not. You're just the good friends I need.'

'You come to our place any time. Dad would have come over but he's stocktaking and Mum's helping and Naveed is out with his mates. But we're all going to live on your doorstep and we hope you're going to live on ours.'

Janata gripped his hand. 'You're great. All of you.'

'We just see you as one of the family. I always wished you'd come to the same secondary school as me.'

Janata hesitated and looked uneasy. 'Maybe it was better that I didn't.'

'Why?' Imran looked at him in genuine surprise and Janata laughed.

'Maybe your mates wouldn't have tolerated a gay for a friend.'

'It wouldn't have made any difference to me.'

'It could have complicated things for you.'

'Life *is* complicated.'

'And as for your dad – '

'What about him?'

'He's fantastic. Like some kind of saint.'

'I've never thought of him like that,' said Imran laughing.

'Well, a strict Muslim like him helping a gay. I mean, they're dead against it, aren't they? Like to have them all tarred and feathered.'

Imran paused. Then he said slowly: 'My dad's the kind of guy who accepts people at face value. That's the kind of bloke he is. And that goes for Mum and Naveed too.'

'What about your girlfriend then?'

'What about her?' Imran was immediately defensive.

'She's white, isn't she?'

'Doesn't make her a villain.'

'No. But what does *she* think?'

'She's fine.'

'What does she think about you coming round to see me?' Janata persisted.

Imran was so taken aback by the unexpected question that he stuttered as he replied, 'She's fine about it all. Absolutely fine.'

Janata looked at him for a moment and then said: 'I don't want to be a burden to you. Make life more complicated for you and your family. Or for you and her.'

'Don't worry,' said Imran firmly. 'You won't.' He changed the subject quickly. 'What do you think about this flat?'

'Bit of a dump, but I can fix it up.'

'I hope you'll let us help.'

Janata nodded a little vaguely. Then he said: 'You can live happily for years with HIV.'

'You bet you can,' replied Imran.

Once he got to the flat Terry slowed up and tiptoed to the window. He paused, bent down and looked inside. At first it was difficult to make out the familiar front room. Then he saw that someone was sitting talking to his parents, and he quickly ducked down for there was something about that person that was depressingly familiar. He peered cautiously in at the window again. Yes, it really was a uniformed police-man. Hurriedly he turned and began to walk quickly away. When he was at a safe distance he burst into a run.

Two

Sharon found Imran in the youth club. For a Saturday night it was not very crowded and he was sitting alone, watching the television. She went straight over to him.

'I'm sorry.'

'Yeah?'

'I'm really sorry.'

Imran turned and grinned affectionately at her. 'That's all right, then.'

'I do hope it is,' she said, surprised by his change of mood.

'What do you mean?'

'I was afraid – that's all.'

'Don't start it up all over again.'

'I'm not.'

Imran stood up and kissed her. 'He's a family friend. The fact that he's got what he's got is neither here nor there. OK?'

Despite their reconciliation Sharon was irritated. What right did he have to be so superior? 'I never said – ' she began defensively.

'So would you like to meet Janata?'

'Of course. When?'

'He's gone to see some mates tonight, but he's going to move into the flat next week. It's pretty lousy, so maybe we could give him a hand decorating it?'

'Sure.' She spoke brightly and quickly and he gave her a suspicious look.

'He's not going to *give* you anything, you know.'

'Listen, Imran,' Sharon began angrily.

'Yeah?'

'I was afraid. I'm sorry.'

'Fear starts prejudice,' he said, and reluctantly she nodded. She still thought he was being frightfully superior.

'I agree. But I can't help being afraid, can I? Maybe you could help me get over it instead of jumping down my throat.'

Immediately Imran took her hand. 'I'm sorry,' he said. 'I don't want to give you a hard time.'

'Let's forget it. What shall we do tomorrow? Can't we do something on our own? Not with the usual old crowd.'

'OK. But we have to be careful.'

'Careful?'

'Some nutter escaped from the hospital this afternoon. Janata told me. He topped his sister or something, and his parents live here. Could be wandering about. Let's have a day out. Go down to Hastings. Yes?'

'Great,' said Sharon, smiling up at him.

Terry sat shivering in the car park that ran under Starling Point. It was a vast open space that was often flooded in winter. Most of the year it was empty, because none of the Starling Point residents would park their cars there for fear of vandalism, so it had become the haunt of kids and vagrants and people sniffing glue or selling drugs. Several times the council had boarded it up, but the fencing was soon broken down and the sinister life style of the car park began all over again.

Terry had tucked himself into the back of a derelict car. It stank of refuse and urine, but it was the only refuge that he could think of and suddenly he was desperately tired. Gradually he fell into a deep sleep and dreamt of wheeling his parents out in their double invalid carriage. Later he dreamt of Tessa. He was on the seashore and she was calling to him and he couldn't find her anywhere. Then he saw a hand waving from the sea and ran towards it. A policeman appeared and began to chase him. Eventually Terry fell over on the beach, and as he felt the handcuffs go on he heard his father shouting abuse at him. It was a familiar dream.

The barbecue began at nine and was a terrific success. The square was packed with people and the local butcher roasted a huge ox on a spit. There were hamburgers and hot dogs and games for the kids and floodlit bingo and a wobbly castle and a fortune-teller. Sharon and Imran, Gallica and Mick, Jonty, Mr and Mrs Dapor, Jonty's mum, old Mrs Willard and hosts of other people that they knew had come, and there was an atmosphere of good-humoured merrymaking. The landlord of the Flag, the pub that was built into the ground floor of Starling Point, had put up an outside bar, and a steel band soon got everyone dancing in the square.

But in one house all was gloom. Mr and Mrs Bonnington sat in the kitchen, leaving the policeman to watch telly in the front room. They felt they had to have some time to themselves for they had already sat with him for hours. He was due to be relieved at ten and then there would be another copper to entertain.

'They should have kept an eye on him,' Mrs Bonnington said as she sat at the table drinking gin.

Arthur Bonnington sighed. She had definitely got herself into a state. There were times when they were beginning to live with the tragedy of their daughter's death but now Terry's absconding had brought it all back. The wound was as raw at this moment as it had been two years ago.

Arthur Bonnington was in his mid-forties, a big jovial man who liked a drink but was still fit. He worked hard at his sports shop, which was dependent on local custom, and was a key figure at the squash club. His son had been a continuous disappointment to him, and now that he had turned into a loony, as he privately called him, he wished that they would keep him in the unit for ever. He was disappointed that the authorities had not committed Terry for life, but what had happened had never been that clear and social workers had said there was a possibility that Tessa might have accidentally drowned and what had seemed to be Terry pushing her under had, in fact, been Terry trying to rescue her. But Mr Bonnington had never thought that very likely, because of Terry's past record.

Over the past two years he had seen his wife Anita gradually deteriorating. She had always been highly strung, and he had given her her head with the dancing to keep her happy, but now, since Tessa, she had buried herself in it. He had been too dependent on the business to move her away from Starling Point, so the gossips had had a field day when Tessa had drowned and Terry had been put away.

'They'll catch up with him,' he said reassuringly. 'He'll try and hitch somewhere.'

'But they obviously think he'll come back here.'

'Well, he won't. He'd know that's where the coppers would look for him, wouldn't he?'

'I don't know. He's not all there, is he? He might just want to be back home with us.' In spite of everything Anita Bonnington had always harboured a far deeper love for her broken son than she had ever let on to her husband. If only she could have managed she would have liked to have him at home, but how could she cope with his violence and the madness that had showed itself in his very early teens? It was right to put him away, but she also felt very guilty about him. Sometimes she feared that Arthur wished him dead, and she couldn't bear to think of that.

She was never sure about the drowning. Perhaps it had been an accident after all. But even an accident had been Terry's fault – he should never have encouraged his sister to swim out with him. But he was her son, still – and she couldn't forget him just because he was locked away.

The tragedy of their children had driven the Bonningtons apart, but now they had been thrown together on a Saturday night when she could have been dancing and he, no doubt, down at the squash club. Instead, here they were, sitting together getting drunk in a sweltering kitchen, with a copper in the front room just in case their loopy son paid them a visit.

As she drank more gin she saw him as a baby and as a little kid. He had been a wonderful child; outgoing and equally good at sport and school work, well-built and the apple of their eye until all the pressure seemed to overtake him when he was twelve and their marvellous son became too mixed-up for them to cope with.

The barbecue and dancing did not end till after two in the morning and it was only then that the residents of Starling Point began to think of going home to bed. It was a beautiful night with a great full moon and a cloudless sky that was ablaze with stars.

'Starling Point looks like a castle, Mick,' said Gallica, clinging to him as he danced on, despite the fact that the band were now packing up and had ceased playing five minutes ago. Mick was a bit the worse for wear, but he was in a good mood and Gallica was happy. Originally they had been thrown together and for a while had only needed each other physically, but now she was beginning to appreciate what a particularly fine person Mick was.

'Call me Michael,' he said as they sat down on the wall that ran round the square.

'Why?' she giggled and then saw that he was serious.

'Mick was the idiot,' he said. 'The berk. The one who was in trouble with the law. The one who was out of work. The one everyone knew was a failure.'

'I can't call you Michael. It's too formal.'

'Well, Mike, then. But not Mick.'

'I'll try,' she said smiling, and knew that she would, for she had seen what a determined effort he had made to break away from his past. He had made such a success of his job at the supermarket that Mr Dapor had appointed him assistant manager. Besides, he was gentle and considerate, and although he still didn't think a lot of himself it was that very vulnerability that made Gallica so fond of him. She still loved Leroy in her heart of hearts, and knew that Mick also knew it, but they both lived in hope that her feelings for him would keep on growing. Certainly after such a lovely evening – even if he was a bit drunk – her affection towards him definitely felt stronger. He was such a good person, she thought. He still spent a lot of time with Mrs Willard, the old lady with the numerous cats he had befriended last year. She had her grandson Jonty and his mum and some more friends now, but the cantankerous old lady had never forgotten his friendship and was as fiercely loyal to Mick as he was to her.

'I'll see you home,' he said, getting to his feet with a slight stagger. 'You can't be too careful tonight.'

'Why?'

'Some nutter might be around. Escaped from a

hospital, Imran told me. And by the way – ' he gave a throaty giggle – 'do you reckon Imran is a bit bent?'

'What on earth do you mean?'

'I saw him going into a flat with a bloke this afternoon. And the bloke looked bent all right. Half-caste sort of guy.'

'Don't be so silly.'

Mick laughed again, but there was something in his laugh that made Gallica faintly uneasy. There was only one flaw in Mick's personality and that was his jealousy of Imran. Mick had been so desperately jealous of him at one stage that he had indulged in a lot of racial abuse, but when he had been down on his luck and in trouble with the police Mr Dapor, Imran's father, had offered him the job at the supermarket. Since then Mick had been good friends with Imran and come to accept that his sister was deeply in love with him. In fact his acceptance had seemed total, and this was the first time Gallica had heard Mick say anything derogatory about Imran. After all, he was going out with her and she was an African. She shrugged. Mick had been drinking and probably – definitely – what he had just said was of absolutely no consequence whatsoever.

'Come on,' she said. 'Maybe *I* should see *you* home. Nutter or no nutter.'

Three

Terry slept on till early morning and then woke stiff and cold and hungry. He felt a wave of despair sweep over him as he realised that he could not go back home and all his plans for a wonderful homecoming were spoilt. It was times like these when he felt at his worst and all the terrible feelings swept over him. The times when things went wrong and he was unhappy. Terry couldn't take things going wrong. It made him get muddled, and now he felt that muddle starting all over again. No longer was Tessa bounding ahead of him, or even there as a spirit leading him on. She was out of reach and he couldn't see her. All he had in his mind was a fixed and rigid photograph of her hand raised in the ocean. She wasn't even waving.

Terry struggled out of the car and leant against it, faint with hunger. He had to find her. He put his hand in his pocket. He had about 75p. He looked at his watch. It was seven on a Sunday morning. He would find some food and then go and find Tessa. Once he had found her, he would find a house. Yes, that's right. He would find his own house and he and Tessa would live together forever and no one would harm them and he would prove to his parents that he could look after her and then they would never have policemen in the front room again.

Jonty got up early to do his paper round. Tired after the barbecue, he yawned widely as he wheeled his bike out of the flats and was surprised to see Sharon walking across the square. It was looking a bit devastated in the early morning sun, what with the remains of the barbecue and all the litter of the previous night. Once he had done his paper round he was going to join a work party and help get it all cleared up.

'Sharon.'

'Hi.'

'Why are you up so early?' Jonty's speech was a flat monotone, but he had become so much a part of the community that everyone had stopped noticing it.

'Couldn't sleep. And it was so sunny. Thought I'd take a walk. Might make an early start on the clearing up. Imran and I are going down to Hastings for the day.' It was their favourite spot and the place where they had made love for the first time. They often went back to the cave above the waterline and lay in each other's arms to remind them of those early precious moments. She felt so happy this morning with all their differences resolved, and although secretly she still felt worried about Janata, she certainly wasn't going to risk letting on to Imran again or even, as much as possible, to herself.

Terry staggered out of the car park, looked round to

make sure that he was unobserved, and then saw that the newsagents was open. He went in and bought as many crisps and chocolate as he could for his 75p, and ate it all very quickly. He had no time to waste. He must find Tessa now, for he had so much to do that morning to make her safe. He turned back to Starling Point, knowing that he was taking a risk but knowing also that he would have to take the risk for Tessa. It was worth it. It would turn out fine in the end, and they would both be reunited with their parents soon. Crunching crisps, Terry began to walk down the bottom walkway. He looked an imposing figure with his height and muscular body and long stride. He was dirty and scruffy by now and he felt it, but once he set up house he would clean himself up and feel fresh again.

Sharon saw him striding along. They were in a narrow alley that led to the outside streets, but she thought nothing of it. He was probably an early workman going to a building site somewhere. There were plenty of those around. Forgetting it was Sunday and all the building sites were deserted, she walked on without a care in the world until she passed him and he gave her a smile. It was an ordinary enough smile but directly he was past her he said: 'Hi, Tess.'

'Eh?' She turned, surprised, and then realised that he was confusing her with someone else.

'I'm not Tess.' She smiled at him, still entirely unsuspicious.

'Hi, Tess.'

A little grain of irritation seized Sharon. He looked

intelligent enough, and he had a nice friendly open smile, so why was he so insistent on thinking that she was someone else?

'I told you. I'm not Tess. My name's Sharon.'

'Yes, but you're Tess.' The conversation was becoming ridiculous and she shrugged and walked on. Maybe he was drunk or something. Yet she still didn't think of running.

'Tess.'

'Go away.'

In a moment he had grabbed her from behind, and she was struggling in his amazingly strong arms. They felt like steel hawsers. Then he clapped a hand that smelt of salt and vinegar crisps over her mouth. She struggled, but he had pinned her so firmly that she did not have one limb free.

'You come with me.'

A wave of panic seized her and over and over again she tried to scream, but his hand was too strong to let her utter a sound.

'I've got a knife in my pocket; if you scream or try and run I'll stick it in you. Right?'

She nodded her head, or tried to. He was so strong, and there was something positive in his voice that made her quite sure he would definitely do as he said.

Slowly he released her and she looked desperately round for help. But there was no one – not even the clatter of the milkman. The place was silent and the sun was shining gently down on them.

He grinned at her. 'We're going for a walk.' He looked across the square towards B block, which was set back behind the shops. Sharon's heart sank. This was the most deserted part of the Starling Point estate. It was used for emergency accommodation and only a few of the flats were in use. Some were boarded up, but many of the boards swung open, damaged by local kids. Sharon knew that this was where Janata was going to have his flat.

'Move.'

'Where?'

'Over to that boarded-up building. And don't try anything silly.'

Once again his voice was so positive that she didn't dare to run for it; all she could hope for was that someone would come. Her heart sank again; the area behind the shops was completely deserted and a little breeze sent an old Mars bar wrapper darting over the broken concrete. She gave a little gasp of fear as he prodded her forward. One of the windows in front of her was gaping open although the door was boarded up.

'Get through there,' he said. 'And fast.'

'No.'

He prodded her again and she could feel something sharp in her back. Without further comment Sharon climbed over the sill and Terry followed. He felt elated. He had found Tessa so quickly.

Jonty pushed his bike up to B block about ten minutes later. Few newspapers had to be delivered here, but there were one or two and he set about struggling with the vast pile of papers that weighed him down more and more each morning. It was becoming a really difficult task to drag the papers round with him, and the shop would have supplied him with a trolley if his round had not been so big. He was stuck with it, and the newspapers seemed to increase in size each Sunday. He got off his bike, looked at his watch and sauntered across the broken concrete. Most of the flats were boarded up and as he was early Jonty decided to have a bit of a rest. He was feeling increasingly tired from the night before and the gentle sunlight looked wonderful to bask in for a few moments.

Inside the flat smelt of old newspapers and urine and fish and chips. Very old fish and chips. There was a lot of rubbish on the floor, but it looked as if someone had been working here recently. There were a couple of builders' benches and the smell of fresh plaster and when Terry idly switched on one of the lights, the bare room was flooded with pale electricity. Perhaps the flat was being prepared for someone. Sharon kept trying to busy her mind with detail, for a gathering and hysterical fear told her that she was about to be raped. Suddenly panic overwhelmed her. She crouched in a corner, almost gibbering at him in her fear and misery.

'Please let me go. Please.'

'No.'

'Please. I won't say anything.'

'I'm not going to hurt you.' He looked at her with a strange intense affection, but it did not reassure her in the least.

'Please let me go.' She began to sob. 'I promise I won't tell on you.' But he was already trying to fix the board back on the window. It went up, leaving just a crack of daylight.

'I'll look after you. See if I don't.'

'What do you mean?'

'Don't cry. Got any money on you?'

'No, I don't think so.'

He came over to her. 'Come on. Have you or haven't you?' There was an edge to his voice as he stood over her, and she hurriedly went through her pockets. She produced just over five pounds in small change and he looked pleased.

'We can live on that for a bit.'

She shook her head and her sobbing redoubled. 'Let me go.'

But he ignored her completely this time, and gazed round the empty space with interest.

'Come on.'

He pulled her to her feet and dragged her into the kitchen. There was a kettle on the stove, and when he looked into one of the cupboards there was a packet of tea and a jar of coffee. There was also a clothes line and his eyes brightened. 'I'm going shopping,' he said.

'I'll come with you,' she said, seizing the opportunity, but he merely grinned.

'You'll try and run away.'

'No.'

'Yes you will. I'm going to tie you up so you can't.'

'Let me come with you. I'll help you.'

'Come here.' He grabbed her wrist, took out his hanky and suddenly stuffed it into her mouth. For a while she thought that she was going to choke, he had stuffed it so deep down her throat. She gagged again and again and thought that she couldn't breathe, but then she realised that she was breathing through her nose and some of the panic passed.

Once he had made sure that the gag was effective, Terry began to tie her up. He had been in the Scouts when he was younger and had always been good at practical things like knots, so he made a good job of trussing her up. He even bound her wrists to her ankles, but he did it quite carefully, so that the circulation wasn't cut off.

'I'll be back soon,' he said, taking her five pounds. Easing the board back down again, he clambered out, leaving her immobile in the kitchen.

Emerging from the flat Terry blinked in the glare of the sunlight. With a shock he saw the newspaper boy asleep on the broken concrete. He looked very peaceful as Terry tiptoed past, and he wondered if he would still be there when he came back. That could be awkward and he wondered what he would be able to do about it. But his one priority now was to get to a shop that was open, stock up and return as quickly as he could. If he was to please his parents he and Tess had to get on with their holiday quickly. The muddled feeling had gone and Terry felt buoyant and optimistic again. He was going on holiday with his sister and they would play on the beach and every day would be sunny and they would come back to the boarding house with sand between their toes and have high tea and go to the fair in the evening. Somewhere his parents were swinging along beside them, but mainly it was him and Tess, alone and happy, and he would prove that he could look after her however silly she got. Of course, the main thing that he had to remember was not to lose his temper, for if he did then all kinds of nasty things happened and his dad would be cross and his mum would cry and there would be a policeman in the living room.

Sharon desperately struggled with her bonds, but it was no good. He had tied them up all too tightly. And the gag was making it difficult for her to breathe again. What was she going to do? He would kill her. The salty tears coursed down her cheeks, and she wept until they would come no more. The panic surged and surged again until she could hardly breathe. If only someone would come. She thought of Imran, calling round in vain for her for their promised day out, and her eyes filled with the few remaining tears that would come. What would he think? Would he in some way link up her non-appearance with the quarrel over Janata? She began to shake from top to toe. Nothing as bad as this had ever happened in her life before. How would she survive it?

Jonty woke and yawned, stretching like a cat in the morning sun. Slowly he got to his feet, feeling rested. He looked at his watch. It was eight. He had been asleep for half an hour and now he was late on his round. Then he saw the pale glow of electricity from the boarded-up window and went over to have a look. Maybe squatters had moved in. They often did. Then he saw something that was vaguely familiar

35

lying on the floor inside the flat. What was it? He bent over the sill to take a closer look and saw that it was a hair comb shaped like a mermaid. Where had he seen that before? Then he realised that the last time he had seen it Sharon had been wearing it. What was it doing here? It must be hers. He'd never seen anyone else wearing one. Instinctively Jonty climbed over the sill.

Imran got up at eight, knowing that he would call on Sharon in an hour and then they would go down to Hastings. It was going to be a super day and he began to hunt for his swimming things. Later on, when they got back, he was going to help Janata to move. They would bring across a few of his things every day. He hoped that Sharon would help, and as a result of last night he felt reassured and supposed that she would. He knew he was being over-protective of Janata and that Janata knew that and was worried. He had to be careful, but he was so anxious that Janata should find happiness with them all at Starling Point and be accepted for what he was as a person. He went down to the kitchen. No one was up and he made some tea for his parents and his brother and took it up to them. When he had done that he sat at the kitchen table and made some toast and looked forward to the day out. He had been going with Sharon for over a year now, and nothing had seriously disturbed their happiness and he was determined that nothing should.

Jonty picked up the comb and looked at it. It could

be anyone's, but the design was so unique it must be hers. He walked on into the other room wondering if anyone was there and tensing his stomach muscles. Because he was deaf his other senses were more acute and he was sure that someone was there. He began to tremble, and when he came into the kitchen he felt that his heart had suddenly stopped. At first he thought that it was a sack or a pile of old clothes lying on the floor near the sink. Then he saw the pile move and recognised it in the gloom.

'Sharon,' he breathed.

Terry felt triumphant as he walked back from the shop, burdened down by his purchases. He had at least enough food for the holiday, and when they got back they could go and eat at his parents'. He had bought bread and bacon and breakfast cereal and a tin of cold meat and some baby tomatoes and biscuits and orangeade. It really should be enough and he had even bought some matches for he couldn't remember if he had seen any in the kitchen. They would be well stocked up and he began to hum a little tune that he used to sing with Tess:

> 'We'll be coming round the mountain when we come.
> We'll be coming round the mountain when we come.
> We'll be coming round the . . . '

He was back in the square and the window was open and he was home again. A feeling of great warmth and happiness flooded him, and Terry almost called out her name. But then he stopped himself for he knew that he had to be careful. Looking round and making sure that he was unobserved, Terry climbed over the sill.

'Hurry.'

Jonty had almost untied her when he stiffened. Only one arm remained tied as he stood there tensely.

'What's happening?' Her voice was a croak and he was looking away from her. She nudged him and repeated the question.

'Someone's here,' he replied.

When Terry came into the kitchen all he could see was the boy crouched over Tess. He was obviously doing her some harm. With a howl of rage he launched himself at him.

Four

Imran knocked on the Newbys' door, and after what seemed like an eternity it was opened by Mick. He looked awful. Over the last year they had become quite friendly, although the previous year Mick had bitterly resented his involvement with Sharon. But Imran always knew that there was an underlying tension between them that he hoped was now on the wane.

'Yeah?'

'I've come for Sharon.'

'She must be in bed.'

Imran sighed. 'I told her I was going to pick her up at nine.'

'Hang on.' Mick disappeared. He was away for about five minutes, during which Imran imagined he was hauling her out of bed. But he returned looking mystified.

'Funny.'

'What's funny?'

'Her bed's made. Maybe she went down the paper shop.'

'Thanks, Mick.'

'My name's not Mick.'

'Eh?' Imran stared at him as if he had gone mad. He must have a hangover, or perhaps he was suffering from amnesia. 'Who are you, then?'

'Mike.'

'Not Mick?'

'I've left him behind. Call me Mike now, or Michael if you like.'

'I'll stick to Mike, Mick. I mean Mike.'

'By the way – '

'Yes?'

'I heard something last night that really worried me.'

'Oh?'

'Yeah. A bloke with AIDS is moving on to the estate.'

'Yes.'

'We can't have that.'

'Why not?' said Imran as mildly as he could. It was ironic that his first test was to be with Mick.

'He could give it to us all.'

'That's impossible. And besides, he hasn't got AIDS. He's just HIV positive.'

'That's the same.'

'It's not,' said Imran and started to explain. But Mick cut him off sharply.

'So he is a mate of yours. I thought I saw you with him.'

'Yes, he is a mate of mine. But I want to explain about this HIV.'

'There's nothing to say. That bloke's not moving in here, I tell you. What about all the little kids?'

'He's harmless. The poor bloke's ill. But he's not likely to pass it on.'

'Course he can. You tell him not to move in here.'

'He's coming. And he's got a perfect right to.'

'Who says? Not in my book, he hasn't.'

'Now look . . .'

'Now you look. This bloke a Paki?'

'He has a Pakistani father and an English mother.'

'A bit of both, is he? So why don't he go home to them? Why don't they see to him?'

'Because he doesn't get on with them.'

'Because he's a queer?'

'Not everyone with HIV is gay.'

'Is he a junkie?'

'As it happens he's gay, but that's no business of yours or mine. He's a nice guy and his parents and my parents are old friends and . . .'

'So he's a nice guy, is he?' scoffed Mick. 'Mr Nice Guy.' He grinned. 'So when do you kiss and make up? AC/DC, are you? Bit of my sister and a bit of him?'

Imran hit him hard in the face and then watched him fall back on the floor, his nose running with blood. He lay there for a moment, staring up at Imran with his eyes full of murder. As he staggered to his feet Mick said, 'I'll get you for that – ' But just as Imran was tensing himself, Mr Newby ran down the stairs in a bright red dressing gown. He took one look at Mick and the blood pouring from his nose, and came straight up to Imran.

'Did you do this to my son?'

'He insulted me.'

'This is about Sharon, is it?' he snapped. 'I thought there was something going on. Where is she?'

'She's gone out to avoid him, Dad.'

'She has not,' yelled Imran. 'I've come to collect her.'

'That's what I mean.' Mick dripped blood on the carpet. 'She's done a bunk.'

'And just why has she done that?' asked Mr Newby.

Imran stepped back, staring at the furious pair of them and realising that in the last five minutes his stock had been reduced to zero. How had it all happened? How had he mishandled it all so badly? He backed away and then turned on his heel.

'I'm going to find Sharon.'

'I forbid you to see her,' said Mr Newby.

'Stuff you,' replied Imran and strode off.

Sharon stared down at Jonty as he lay on the floor at Terry's feet. Terry hadn't hit him but had picked him up and thrown him halfway across the kitchen. Now he stood over him panting.

'Who is he?'

'He's Jonty. And he's deaf. You can see his deaf aids.'

Terry looked down and saw that there was one on each ear. Neither had come out. Jonty was staring up at him, looking dazed.

'He shouldn't have come.'

'Then let him go,' said Sharon.

'If I let him go he'll tell. Won't you?' said Terry in

a sing-song voice that was terrifying to hear. 'You'll tell.'

'No I won't.'

'You'll have to stay here with me and Tess, at least until the holiday is over. And you're not to spoil it.' He moved over to them. 'I'm going to tie you two together until you learn to behave.' He sounded like one of the nurses at the hospital who had once put him in a jacket thing that he couldn't move in and had said roughly the same thing.

Jonty scrambled to his feet but Sharon said. 'No, Jonty.'

Jonty couldn't hear, or didn't seem to want to. He hurled himself at Terry, kicking and punching at him, but Terry just gently held him off.

'I'll have to hurt you in a minute,' he said. Jonty stopped struggling and stood there hopelessly. Then he went over to Sharon who was still hunched up on the floor. He sat down beside her.

'For the last time,' said Sharon desperately. 'Let us go. You'll be in terrible trouble with the police if you keep us here.'

But Terry didn't seem to be listening at all. He began to hum and then to sing as he methodically tied them both together with the clothes line.

> 'We'll be coming round the mountain when we come.
> We'll be coming round the mountain when we come.
> We'll be coming round the mountain . . . '

He broke off as he lashed their ankles together.

'That's our favourite song, isn't it, Tess?' He smiled and ruffled her hair. 'Don't worry. This is going to be a super holiday.' He bent his head next to Jonty's. 'You know what?'

'What?'

'You're not to spoil it.' Then Terry was struck by a sudden thought. 'You are silly,' he said to Jonty.

'Why?'

'Well, you didn't bring your share of the food, did you? Got any money on you?'

'No.'

Terry went through Jonty's jacket pocket and found three pounds. 'You are silly,' he repeated. 'You must have forgotten all this. I'll have to go back to the shop. Then we can start our holiday.'

He stood up and pocketed the money. For a moment he was worried. If Jonty had come, suppose somebody else did. Then Terry made up his mind that he would have to take the risk. After all, it would spoil the holiday if they didn't have enough to eat. Holidays were meant to be fun, and this one was going to be great and if this boy had to share it, well he would have to sit in another room. It was his own fault. He wanted to be with Tess on her own after all this time, and he would, too.

Whistling his unbearable tune, Terry left the room, pulled back the board, looked around him and then climbed out into the sunshine. He replaced the board and then hurried away, still whistling.

'You stocking up, son?' asked the owner of the small shop a couple of streets away from Starling Point that Terry had returned to for the second time that morning.

'I'm on me holidays,' said Terry, and beamed at him. Odd, thought the man as he rang up for two pounds of sausages and some cooking fat.

'I'm staying with me sister,' said Terry, paying for the goods.

'That's nice,' the man replied.

Imran was searching the estate for Sharon. He felt thoroughly rattled and wished to God that he hadn't lost his temper. Now he had made the situation much worse. Maybe he should go back and apologise. But then he thought of Mr Newby, and Mick in his present mood, and dismissed the idea from his mind. He had tried to explain about Janata. Where had he gone wrong? He thought of all the filthy things that Mick had said and wanted to hit him all over again. He would have liked to have hit Mr Newby too. And as for calling Mick, Mike – Mick was the same old Mick that ever he was, however much he had come up in the world, and Imran wondered why he had been fooled for one moment. But the main thing that was pressing on his mind more than anything else was where in the hell was Sharon? Could she have walked out on him? Could she be deliberately avoiding him? Had Mick poisoned her mind against him? But how? They had had a wonderful time at the barbecue and she had understood. Surely she had understood? And Imran went on searching with an increasingly heavy heart.

Mick was very sorry for what he had done and was not surprised that Imran had hit him. He had woken up with a terrible hangover, and his old self had come back. He had tried so hard to be friendly with Imran, and he had succeeded for the last year, until now. It wasn't Imran's colour, and although he was worried about the new resident at Starling Point he wasn't that worried. He was very happy with Gallica, although he felt sure it couldn't last. Perhaps that had made him lash out: the deep-down jealousy he still felt for the fact that Imran and Sharon were so happy together. He was slowly making something of his life, he knew that, and he had been bursting with pride to be made an assistant manager at the supermarket. He hadn't even felt patronised that it was Imran's family who had given him the job. It was just that he had a strong feeling that Gallica could walk out on him any time — particularly if Leroy turned up on the scene again. He was fatalistic about it, and today he had awoken with a hangover and lashed out.

Now he had caused the most amazing damage and dragged his father into it — a man that he loathed and had no respect for at all. Of course, his father had been only too pleased, and had just spent the last ten minutes in a mood of euphoric righteous indignation. Soon his mother would be down to join in, and his hangover was getting worse by the minute. And, of course, if Gallica found out what he had said and done, and she probably would because she was very friendly with Imran and Sharon, she would be furious. Mick covered his face with his hands as he heard his mother begin to make her grumbling descent.

When Terry got back his two prisoners were still tied up and no other visitors had arrived. He dumped the food down and ungagged them, even feeling more friendly towards Jonty.

'It's going to be a super holiday, Tess,' he said as he filled the kettle. 'I'm going to give you a real treat. We'll go for a walk on the beach and then we'll have bangers for lunch. You can stay for that and then you'll have to go in another room,' he said to Jonty quite kindly.

'How are we going to walk on the beach tied up?' asked Sharon. She felt a fraction less frightened, and she had tried to reassure Jonty with her eyes while Terry had been out. If she could talk to him then maybe he would let them go. He was obviously quite potty and would be very dangerous if thwarted. The great thing to do was not to thwart him.

'I'll untie you if you're going to behave,' he said as if to a naughty child. 'But not you,' he added admonishingly to Jonty. 'I'm not having both of you running about being silly.'

'When can we go for the walk?' asked Sharon.

'Now,' said Terry.

'Untie me then.'

'Oh, I don't have to do that. Look, there's the beach and the tide's out.' He was looking at a blank wall and Sharon's heart sank. She looked at Jonty and he shook his head. Terry was madder than they had both thought. They were going to have a holiday in his mind.

Five

'Imran.'

He was sitting dejectedly in the square. It was ten and a few of the Starling Point residents were going through the motions of attempting to clear up the debris. But no one was very enthusiastic about it. Mick walked slowly towards him and Imran groaned. Now he would have to fight him, and he didn't feel in the least like doing so. A public fight in the square on a Sunday morning would get them both into deep trouble, but he knew that he couldn't walk away from it. Reluctantly he stood up, but when he looked at Mick he saw with surprise that he was looking extremely unhappy.

'What do you want?'

'Say I'm sorry.'

'*What*?' Imran was at a complete loss for words. Sorry? Mick?

'I had a hangover. I deserved what I got.'

'Blimey.'

'So maybe my name's still Mick.' He gave Imran a shamefaced grin and held out his hand.

Imran took it, staring at him. 'You sure?'

'Yeah.'

'After all you said?'

'I'm really sorry for what I said about you. I didn't mean it. I was scared about that bloke, that's all. But he's got a right to his life and the way he wants to lead it. We all have.'

Imran still gaped at him. 'I didn't handle it very well myself,' he said at last. 'I'm sorry about belting you.'

'I deserved all I got,' Mick repeated. 'Only pity was it got Dad going and now Mum's raving. They never got used to you and Sharon and this has just stirred them up.'

'Shall I come and apologise?'

'No. Let me try and sort it. It's more my mess than yours. And if this boy friend of yours – ' he grinned – 'I mean this mate of yours, wants a hand then let me help.'

'Are you still suspicious about him?'

'No. I was scared, I guess. That's the way it takes a lot of people. They're pig-ignorant, you see.'

'I really respect you for saying all this.'

'Meaning?'

'Meaning just that.'

'What you really mean is that a year ago I'd have been a Paki-basher and a queer-basher and anything else I didn't like or was afraid of -basher. Right?'

'Maybe. But you're not now, Mike. Or would you prefer Michael?'

'I wouldn't mind Michael,' he said and grinned. 'And now do you want a hand trying to find that sister of mine?'

Half an hour later they met Gallica who looked tired and anxious. When they explained things to her she looked even more worried.

'I've just been speaking to Jonty's mum. He didn't come back from his newspaper round and now they've found his bike on B block.'

'Who found it?'

'Some other kids. She doesn't know whether to call the police or not. Do you remember that time when his dad kidnapped him?'

'His dad's inside now,' said Mick.

'Maybe he got out,' she said.

'No!'

'What's up?' they chorused, shocked by Imran's anguished cry.

'That bloke.'

'What bloke?' said Gallica.

'The nutter. The one Janata told me about. The one that escaped. Maybe he's grabbed Sharon – and Jonty.'

They stared at each other in dawning horror.

'Where did you say that bike was?' asked Imran.

'By B block. You know, the emergency bit,' said Gallica.

'That's where your friend's living, isn't he?' asked Mick.

'Meaning?' asked Imran fiercely.

'Nothing,' said Mick quickly.

'He's not even moved in yet.'

'All right,' said Mick. 'The main thing is to get there fast.'

'Shouldn't we ring the police?' asked Gallica.

'Let's just check it out first,' said Mick.

It was half past ten by the time they arrived at B block, and at first sight it seemed to be as ordinary and as semi-derelict as ever. It was one of the tower blocks that no one would really want to live in. The emergency flats were on the lower storeys and the higher floors were empty. Moves had been made to have the entire block pulled down, but although it had been much discussed nothing ever happened, and the empty floors were left to deteriorate. Popular rumour had it that they were full of monster rats scrabbling at the blocked-off doorways, anxious to get out and feed off the residents.

On the lower floors the windows were often boarded up and squatters had moved in on the other side of the tower. It was a wasteland now and its dereliction was depressing. One or two of the emergency residents had tried to brighten the place up with a tub or two of flowers, but even these seemed to emphasise the litter and the broken concrete.

'Doesn't look like anyone's been around for a long time,' said Mick as he gazed at the boarded-up doorways on the south side of the tower. Then he saw that one of the boards at the window had come loose and was showing a metre or so of clear space. Then Imran saw something else.

'There's steam coming out of there,' he said.

The kettle had almost boiled itself dry as Terry talked, and still he hadn't noticed. Jonty and Sharon were too afraid to interrupt him in full flood. There was something passionate about the way Terry was

52

talking – passionate and hypnotic – and they could both almost see and smell the beach and hear the sea. He would have made a wonderful story-teller, thought Jonty as he watched Terry's lips move gently through his re-creation of the holiday.

'There we go. Let's get into that sea. It'll be a bit shallow when we get in, but if we run we'll soon be up to our waists. It's not so cold now, is it? Here we go.' He gave a shout of joy and Sharon closed her eyes and felt the water gradually creeping up around her. It was cold but the sun was warm on her back. Somewhere ahead of her she saw Terry, and when she turned on to her side she could see that Jonty was running alongside her. She could feel the water getting deeper and then suddenly she was laughing and screaming. Once you got used to it it was lovely and warm, and she could see that Terry was turning and was swimming his way back towards her. Jonty was a little behind them, swimming on his own. Terry splashed her and said: 'Isn't it great?'

'It's lovely,' she seemed to say.

'Aren't you pleased you came in?'

'You bet.'

'We're going to have a smashing holiday.'

'You bet,' she repeated.

'Let's swim out a bit.'

'I don't want to go out of my depth.'

'You'll be fine.'

'No.'

'You'll be fine.'

Sharon tried to pull herself together. Was she so very tired or shocked or something? For a few seconds she really had been out there in the sea and she was frightened. No, she didn't want to go out of her depth, and Terry was still asking her to do so, only now she was sitting on the hard floor trussed up to Jonty.

'Come on. You'll be OK out of your depth. You'll be all right with me.'

'Is anyone there?' The voice seemed to be coming from a different world. Then she recognised it as Mick's and stiffened. So did Jonty.

'Is anyone there?'

The steam in the kitchen was thick and she could see it drifting through to the other room.

'Is anyone there?'

'Who's that?' Terry whipped round, his face suddenly stripped of all its happiness.

'Is anyone there?'

'You stay there.'

'I'm coming in,' said Mick.

Sharon could hear battering at the boarding round the window and began to scream for help.

'It's OK,' said Mick. 'I'm coming in.'

Sharon and Jonty both began to yell as loudly as they could. Meanwhile Terry had rushed into the other room.

'Stop,' he said authoritatively.

There was a brief silence. Then they could hear Gallica's voice saying: 'What's going on?'

'Go away,' said Terry briskly.

'Do you have Sharon and Jonty in there?'

'Yeah.'

'What are you doing with them?'

'They're having a holiday with me,' said Terry firmly.

'It's him,' Sharon heard Mick mutter. 'The loony.'

'What did you call me?'

'Nothing,' said Imran. He sounded amazingly calm. 'We've come to fetch Sharon and Jonty – they have to leave now. We're going out.'

'They're already out. Out with me.'

'Yes, but they have to go now.'

'They're not going anywhere. They're on holiday with me. And we're having a great time. Aren't we?' he called back.

'Help!' screamed Sharon. 'For God's sake, help us.'

'We are,' said Mick. 'Come on, let's rush him.'

She could hear the board being bashed again and then Terry saying, 'You come in and I'll kill them.'

There was another dead silence. Then Mick said very softly, 'What did you say just then?'

'You come any nearer and I'll kill them. I've got a knife and I'll kill them. You see if I don't.' His voice suddenly rose to a sob. 'You can't just come in and spoil my holiday.'

Sharon waited to see what they would do. She felt curiously numb. Jonty meanwhile was terrified. He had barely got used to Terry's suspended childhood, and this sudden development was too much for him. He began to cry as Terry untied Sharon and took her through to the next room.

Outside the three of them held a whispered consultation.

'Get the police,' whispered Gallica.

'Wait,' said Imran. 'We need to calm him down first. We have to reassure him.'

'I still say we should try and rush him,' said Mick but there was doubt in his voice. He and Gallica both looked at Imran, recognising that he was now their leader, impressed by his calm.

'I want to talk to him, to calm him down. And then we should get some help.' He moved to the window.

'Hallo.'

There was no reply.

'Hallo.'

There was only a scuffling sound, but through the gap at the top of the window he could just make out Sharon's face. Her eyes were puffy from crying and she was dead white. Behind her he could see a man. He was big and there was something in his eyes that convinced Imran that he was crazy. He was like a big sulky child in a man's body, and his eyes had the malice of a thwarted child.

'Here she is,' said the man triumphantly.

'What's your name?' asked Imran quietly.

'Not telling you.'

'Please.'

'My name's Terry. And I'm on holiday with my sister Tessa and another boy.'

Gallica felt a sudden chill and she saw that Mick had closed his eyes. Knowing Mick and his temper and his worship of Sharon, she wondered just how long he would follow Imran's softly-softly approach.

'We're not trying to spoil your holiday,' said Imran gently. 'We just want to share it.'

It was immediately obvious that was not the right thing to say.

'I don't want anyone to share it,' said Terry petulantly. 'It's just for my sister and me. And then this other boy turned up. It's not fair. It's her and me only, and my parents have to know that I can look after her all right.' His voice was childish now and Imran dimly realised that Terry was regressing by the minute.

'Sorry.'

'Go away, then.'

'OK, we will. But you're not to hurt her.'

'What?'

'I said, please don't hurt her.'

'Me? Hurt Tess? I'll bleedin' well hurt you. You come in here and I'll kill you.' His voice was no longer the voice of a child but a ruthless adult, and it was terrifying to hear. Even Mick looked shaken.

'Come on,' he whispered and made telephoning gestures.

'Don't upset him,' said Sharon suddenly. 'He's a really good brother to me.'

'Eh?' Mick jumped forward but Imran grabbed at him as Gallica tried to kick him and missed.

'I know that you don't mean any harm,' said Sharon. She was speaking very slowly. 'But everyone has got to be nice to Terry.'

Terry nodded his head and grinned behind her.

'She's right,' he said. 'It's about time everyone was nice. Hey, tell you what – '

'Yes?' Imran tried to sound relaxed, but he was trembling now and was not sure how long he could

57

keep his voice normal. Then he looked at Sharon and drew courage from her.

'Why don't you go shopping for us? I didn't have much money. Get us some more food and we can have a longer holiday.'

Gallica nodded at him and Imran said, 'Fine. What would you like?'

'I'd like some fish and chips. That's seaside food. Would you like some fish and chips, Tess?'

'Yes, please.'

'Go and get them,' he ordered. 'And be quick about it.'

'We won't be long,' said Imran. 'Have a good time.' He began to walk away and the others followed. They reached the stairs and hurried down them.

'Let's get to the nearest phone box,' said Imran. 'We'll call the police.'

'Sure,' said Mick. He paused. 'There's someone else we could call.'

'Who?'

'Your mate. The one who's the nurse at the hospital where this nutter came from. He was his nurse, wasn't he? That's what you said. Couldn't he talk him down?'

'He might make him worse,' said Gallica.

Imran thought it was worth a try, but when he phoned Janata there was no reply, so he immediately phoned the police. They were very efficient and in twenty minutes a squad car had arrived and was drawn up in the Starling Point square. They were very discreet and there had been no sound of sirens.

A small crowd gathered as Gallica, Imran and Mick stood by the car. Inside was Reg, their local policeman, sitting on the back seat, looking very unlike his usual joky self. His face was set and he simply rapped out: 'Where is he?'

Imran told him.

'OK. He's dangerous. You realise that?'

'We know.'

'I'm just waiting for a colleague; he specialises in this kind of situation. We've contacted the boy's parents, Mr and Mrs Bonnington, and they'll be here shortly. Who's he holding?'

'Jonty and Sharon,' said Imran, his voice trembling.

Six

The colleague who specialised in sieges arrived within half an hour. He was middle-aged and Reg introduced him as Inspector Tate. He looked kind and tired and spoke slowly and quietly. After he had questioned them all closely about exactly what Terry had said he nodded and closed his notebook.

'The boy is very sick. I've already spoken to the hospital. We just need to talk him down before he does anything silly.'

'What do you know about him?' asked Imran bluntly.

Inspector Tate paused. 'I wouldn't normally tell you any of this, but I know how much you want to help and there's every reason to think that you can. He was sent to the Victoria because of a drowning incident with his sister, but he has a long history of extreme violence when provoked.'

Imran explained about Janata. 'I think they had a good relationship,' he concluded, and gave the number to Reg who said they would contact him.

By now a crowd had gathered and Mr and Mrs Bonnington had to push their way through. They looked confused and shaken but everyone else took an immediate dislike to them. Mr Bonnington seemed full of bluster and his wife took refuge in giving the impression of being the frightened little thing that Gallica was sure she was not.

'Look here,' began Mr Bonnington. 'My son is mentally ill and I cannot be held responsible for his actions. It's all the fault of the hospital. He should have been in a locked ward, then there would have been no chance of him absconding in this – '

But Inspector Tate held up a weary hand to stem the flood of justification and righteous indignation.

'Just a minute, sir. Are you able to talk to your son?'

'I have no influence on him whatsoever. He killed my daughter. Our daughter. I mean, don't you know that – '

Again Inspector Tate held up a restraining hand. He turned to Mrs Bonnington, who was standing there clutching at her husband's hand and trying to look as beaten down as possible. But Gallica felt instinctively that of the two she was the stronger personality.

'Can *you* talk to your son, madam?'

She shook her head. 'He's very disturbed.' She made a little pinched mouth and Gallica, despite all her worry for Sharon and Jonty, could very cheerfully have kicked her.

'So you can't reach him?'

Again she shook her head. Again the little fearful pinched mouth.

Inspector Tate sighed. 'You do realise that this is a very serious situation, madam. Your son has

61

barricaded himself into an empty flat and claims to be holding two young people at knife point.' But he was interrupted by the arrival of the Newbys as well as Jonty's mother.

'He's going to be busy,' said Mick as the voices increased in argumentative volume. The crowd began to press forward and a journalist arrived from the local paper. He had already tipped off the national press and a couple of television stations and was well pleased with the amount of money he would get. Sunday, the journalist thought, had really brightened up.

In B block Terry had made a more effective job of blockading the window. There was still a small gap through which he could speak and see anyone who came near, but he had wedged the boarding so that it would be difficult to knock down in a hurry. He had also tied up Sharon and Jonty again and checked their bonds. He looked at his watch: it was almost one o'clock. It was quite cool in the dank and shuttered flat, but outside the sun was streaming down. Terry felt more secure now, and was confident he could continue his holiday with greater peace of mind. Sharon and Jonty were very quiet and the fish and chips hadn't turned up yet.

'I hope they're coming back with that grub,' he said. 'It's getting late.' His voice rose a little and Sharon hastened to reassure him.

'There's always a queue on a Sunday,' she said as casually as she could. She prayed they would reappear soon, for she was beginning to realise that it was the little things that wound Terry up. And in these circumstances little things could easily flare up into big things.

'So if you said you'd take them fish and chips let's do that. I'll introduce myself and then we can start negotiations. I've already got the place surrounded, so we've done everything we can so far.'

Imran was really getting to like Inspector Tate. He was calm and reassuring, and had obviously had a lot of experience.

'Do you reckon you can talk him down?'

'In time. But they're all different. I can't predict anything.'

Imran respected him even more for saying that. He was neither aloof nor, thank goodness, prepared to give them any bullshit. He treated them as equals.

'By the way, let's drop the surnames. My name's Ian,' he said and Mick smiled at him gratefully.

Janata walked down the hospital drive in a sombre mood. He had not felt very well today, and staying with a friend and having a late night had not helped either. At twenty-three he felt without energy and very lonely. It was not as if his friends had dropped him. It was not as if he was the only person with HIV. There were plenty of others in his position and of these Janata knew quite a few himself. It was just the awful realisation that he could die. It was not absolutely certain; he didn't have a time limit on his life – but he knew it was a very real danger and he was both afraid and resentful. Afraid because he was afraid of death and the process of dying, and resentful because his family no longer wanted him. His father had rejected him on the grounds that homosexuality was condemned as a great sin by true followers of Islam, and HIV and AIDS were seen as the wages of that sin. He also knew that his father had quarrelled with the Dapors. 'He is not a true Muslim,' he had heard him say to his mother. 'He is condoning what Janata does.' It was almost as if, having made a mixed marriage himself, he was determined to compensate for it by being ultra-orthodox in other ways. His mother had pleaded long and hard on his behalf and she still sent him presents and came to see him at the hospital, but there was no chance of him going home ever. Still he hoped that she would come and see him at his new flat on the Starling Point estate.

Starling Point, he reflected, was the only other bright spark in his life; the loving loyalty of the Dapors and Imran touched him deeply. He was still worried that he would be a nuisance and that Imran would soon be in trouble with his girlfriend or his mates. But they had thrown him a lifeline and he had no other option but to take it.

As he turned into the reception area of the hospital a colleague rushed up to him.

'The police want you.'

'What?' Janata's heart sank. Now what had happened? He wondered for a moment if they wanted him in connection with his lifestyle. But he knew that he had done nothing illegal.

'The Bonnington boy's turned up.'

'Where?'

'He's holed up on the Starling Point estate. Taken some hostages. Girlfriend of someone you know.'

'Who?'

'Daper? Is it Dapor?'

'Dapor. God, no.'

'They want you to go down there.'

'I'm on my way. Reckon I may be able to talk him down.'

'Well, that's what they want.'

'We brought you the fish,' yelled Imran into the gap at the top of the window. There was no reply and he repeated the statement. After a while he heard Terry coming.

'Who's that?'

'We brought you the fish.'

'You were a long time.'

'There was a queue.'

'OK. Pass it in,' said Terry in a less suspicious voice.

'I'm not sure if I can reach.'

'Oh yes you can.'

'I've got someone else who would like a chat.'

'Who?'

'Bloke called Ian.'

'Who is he?'

But Ian was already standing so that he could see through the gap.

'Terry Bonnington?' he said.

'You a copper?'

'Yes.'

'Go to hell.'

'Just wanted a bit of a chat. Your dad and mum are nearby.'

'Are they?'

'Yes. They're looking forward to seeing you soon.'

'Are they?'

'Yes.'

'Promise?'

'Yes.'

'I want to speak to them.'

'Why not? Why don't you come out and have a chat?'

'You don't get me out that way.'

'In your own time.'

'Go to hell.'

'Listen, Terry. Do you want to see your dad and mum?'

'I want to speak to them. Yes. But I'm not coming out. See?'

'OK. So I'll bring them over.'

'Wait a minute.'

'Yes?'

'They'll stand out there. They're not coming in. Not yet. They're not ready to come on holiday with me yet. They might be cross.'

'Oh, I shouldn't think they would be. But I'll bring them along and you can have a talk with them standing out here.'

'I don't like coppers.'

'Not many people do,' Ian joked. 'But we're human, you know.'

'You been sitting in my front room all day and all night waiting to catch me?'

'No. I'm not that copper.'

'Sure?'

'Yeah. Enjoy your fish and chips.'

'You going away?'

'Only to get your mum and dad. That's what you want, isn't it?'

'Yeah. You got marksmen on the roof?'

'Oh no. It's not that kind of situation.'

'I got a knife.'

'Have you?'

'Yeah. Maybe you need them marksmen.'

'You don't want to get hurt, Terry. Not while you're on holiday. Do you?'

'If I get hurt I'll hurt someone else. Like these two. And the boy will get it first. Not my sister.'

'So you got your sister in there with you.'

'What of it?'

'What's her name?'

'Tess.'

'Oh yes. That's nice for you. What are you doing?'

'I told you, stupid, having a holiday. I'm looking after her.'

'You do that. You really look after her. Give her a nice time on that holiday of yours.'

'Don't worry, copper. I will.'

'Why don't you call me Ian?'

'What for?'

'Just to be friendly. We might do a bit of talking, you and me.'

'I don't want to talk to you, copper.'

'We'll see. I'm going to get your mum and dad now.'

Ian turned away and walked back to where Reg was standing with Imran, Gallica and Mick. The area had been cordoned off and a ring of policemen were standing around the base of the tower block. A huge screen was being erected so the siege could not be seen by the increasing crowd. In the square a couple of ambulances and a fire engine waited with half a dozen police cars and a big police bus.

'Well?' asked Reg.

'I'm going to try and do a bit of manipulation.'

'How's that, Ian?'

'He wants his parents. But they're pretty useless anyway. So I'm going to go away for a bit and then come back and say that they don't want to see him unless he releases his sister.'

'His sister? Oh yes, I see what you mean. He's a fantasy merchant, isn't he?'

'A very dangerous one. I want him treated very gently. No surprises. No sudden movements. I want it to be peaceful for as long as we can keep it that way.'

'What happens if he won't deliver the girl?'

'Then we're in trouble.'

'By the way, the nurse is on his way. The one he gets on with.'

'Then we'll hold him in reserve.'

'Fine.'

'Can we speak to them? Cheer them up?' said Gallica.

'No. He thinks your friend Sharon is his sister. He's very disturbed and has a dangerous reputation.
68

We have to keep that fantasy going for as long as we can.'

Seven

'Why don't you untie us?' asked Sharon. 'We can't eat fish and chips like this.'

'I'm going to untie your hands, that's all.'

Sharon noticed that there were two levels with Terry. On the one hand he seemed to be totally convinced that she was Tessa; on the other he was completely aware of the siege and determined to keep them captive for his own ends. These two levels seemed to be completely separate and yet dependent on each other.

Sharon took some of the fish and chips and so did Jonty, but she could see that eating them was as nauseous to him as it was to her. But Terry himself was eating greedily and noisily.

'What shall we do this afternoon?'

'What do you want to do?' asked Jonty, trying to humour him. But Terry was annoyed that he had spoken at all.

'You'll be going into the other room this afternoon,' he said. 'We don't want you interfering, do we, Tess?'

'Let him stay.'

'So you don't want me on my own?' He sounded petulant again and she hastened to reassure him.

'But I thought that we might take a picnic somewhere and Jonty could carry it and lay it all out.' She looked desperately at Jonty, making sure that he had lip-read her. It was never safe to assume he had heard.

He said: 'I'll help in any way you like.'

Terry nodded, temporarily appeased.

'Where shall we go?' asked Sharon. 'Where shall we go with our picnic?'

'We could go on the pier. Or we could go to that rocky cove and scramble down and have it there. There's never anyone there. But that's where you . . . ' His voice petered out.

'Where I what?'

'Where you got into a bit of trouble in the deep water. Where I rescued you.'

'Oh, I'm not afraid any more,' she said.

'OK.' He turned to Jonty. 'All right, you can come,' he said with his mouth full of fish and chips.

'All right,' said Jonty.

'Anyone there?' The policeman's voice was friendly.

Terry trundled out, still eating, to hear what he had to say. I hope to God it's something that he wants to hear, thought Sharon. She winked at Jonty.

'It's going to be all right,' she said. 'The police have got everything under control.'

'So it's just a matter of time,' said Jonty hopefully.

Sharon nodded. 'Just a matter of time.'

But neither felt very reassured.

'Terry.'

'I'm here.'

'Bit of a problem.'

'What?' His voice went hard.

'Your mum and dad are a bit cross about you staying in that flat all the time. They want to see you and Tess outside.'

'You said you'd bring them.'

'They won't come.'

'They're cross.'

'They won't be if you come out. Only if you stay inside.'

'I want to see them.'

'I told you, they won't come.'

'Then I'll hurt someone.'

'Sorry?'

'I'll hurt someone.'

'I wouldn't do that, Terry.'

'Bring them.'

'They – '

'I'll hurt the kid. I'll hurt him bad.'

'Wait.'

Terry's voice rose to a shrill scream. 'I'll hurt him bad.'

In the kitchen Sharon and Jonty huddled together. So much for their brave reassurance.

'I'll hurt him.'

'No, Terry.'

'You see.'

'OK. I'll get them.'

'Promise?'

'I promise.'

'And Ian – ' Inspector Tate felt a slight ray of hope at Terry's use of his christian name.

'Yes?'

'Tell them not to be cross.'

That afternoon Terry took them down to the bay, and again he talked them through – or was it into? – the actual experience itself. It was remarkable how he was able to do it, thought Sharon. Jonty felt the same, except that he was much more afraid than she was. Somehow they could touch the Cornish rocks they were scrambling down, and smell the seaweed on the small boulder-strewn beach. They could also smell the sea and hear the pounding of the waves and feel the hard rock under their feet. Perhaps it's because I'm so tired, thought Sharon, but she didn't want to close her eyes. She kept them wide open. As he talked she forgot the damp-stained walls of the flat, and could only see what Terry was describing. He was willing it on them with all the force of his mad obsession, and he was taking them with him every step of the way. Tied together, with their bonds hurting, Sharon and Jonty lay on the floor in the cool shadowy room and listened to Terry, whose voice was burning bright, confident and clear.

'This beach is a bit rocky but we can take our shoes off here and have a swim, Tess. There's nothing to be frightened about. The sea's lovely and calm out there. It's hot in the sun, isn't it, Tess? But it'll be lovely and cool in the water. Don't worry about being out of your depth. I'll look after you, and if you get tired you can lie on your back and have a rest and

I'll hold you up. It's only the edge that's a bit choppy, and if you hang on to me I'll steer you round the worst of the rocks. But watch out, it gets deep very quickly.

'Here we go. It's only cold at first! You'll soon be OK, Tess. Hang on. Watch out for that big one. It's going to burst all over us and push us back a bit. Here we go again. Now it's all right. Did you bump your leg, Tess? You'll be OK. Look, we're almost out of all the deep water and into the calm. We're in the calm now. Can't you feel it, Tess? Lovely calm water, holding us up, pushing us on. We're going to head for the island. I know it's a long way, but we'll make it. If you get tired I'll give you a nice rest. Here we go. These slow rolling waves are fantastic, aren't they? They're carrying us to the island without having to do any work.

'Look, there's Dad and Mum on the next beach. Let's wave to them, shall we? What's that? You want to swim back to them now? Oh come on, Tess. Let's try and make the island. Come with me. Don't go back to them. Of course we'll make it. We've *got* to make it, haven't we? Just us two. Come on. Don't be chicken and go back to them. You'll never make it on your own anyway.'

Suddenly the joy was over, and when Sharon looked at Jonty she could see that he had been terrified all along. Something was going to happen. She could feel it. Terry was standing totally still, staring at the wall. And in his eyes she could read a finality that made her flesh creep.

Janata had arrived and was immediately fully briefed by Imran with many interruptions from Mick and Gallica. The four of them hung round the police incident post until Imran eventually managed to attract Ian's attention.

'Janata's here and he has an idea,' said Imran abruptly.

Ian wondered why he couldn't speak for himself.

'You're his spokesman, are you?'

Janata intervened, speaking so softly that they could barely hear him.

'I would like to talk to his parents. I know Terry so well and maybe I could – encourage them to give us more help.'

'They certainly need some prompting,' replied Ian sourly. 'They've gone home again and we're running out of time.' Terry's parents and their lack of involvement were making Ian have the very worst forebodings about the outcome of the siege.

'I think I might be able to do some good.'

'Give it a swing,' said Mick and Ian looked at him irritably.

'All right. Let me make the decisions.' He turned back to Janata. 'You reckon you could persuade them to co-operate? Because right now, they're a dead loss and we just don't have time on our side.'

'I think I might be able to get them to talk to him, particularly if I manage to reassure them. I know him very well and *I* never believed that he drowned his sister. I realise how urgent it all is – but if I can get them to speak to him – ' Janata sounded confident and Ian's hopes rose although he knew there was no evidence for optimism.

'You taking this lot with you?' asked Ian disapprovingly.

'I'd rather go alone,' Janata replied firmly.

Ian looked at Mick and suddenly smiled.

'What are you grinning about?' said Mick indignantly. 'I'm a very tactful bloke.'

They all laughed – even Mick. It was as if they hadn't laughed for years, and it temporarily took the pressure off.

'I'll go down with you,' said Ian. 'The Bonningtons need as much pressure as we can give.'

'Don't swim back. Not now. We're nearly there.' Terry's voice rose higher in his agitation. 'Come with me. I can get you to the island. Honest. You don't want to swim back to them.'

Suddenly Jonty cried out in spontaneous terror; he could feel his mouth full of salt water. All Sharon could see were the steeply rising crests of the waves.

'Don't keep yelling.' Terry's voice was still rising. It merged with the booming of the sea and the sound filled the room, drowning everything. Then they heard his voice again. 'You're safe with me. You can't go to them now. Look how near the island is. We *have* to get to the island. Stop struggling. If you struggle you'll go under and that won't do. Listen to me. You *can't* swim back to the beach. It's too far. You won't make it. Swim to the island. With me. Stop struggling, Tess. Tess. You're going under. You're going under, Tess. I'm trying to help you.

Look, Mum and Dad are standing up on the beach. You'll get me into trouble if you go under again. Honest you will, Tess. Tess. Hang on to me. Hang on to me. They're waving. They're coming. Dad's swimming out. Tess. Tess, where are you? Where are you?'

His voice ended on a long anguished howl that was dreadful to hear, and Sharon and Jonty could feel the salt water flooding into their mouths and rushing down the back of their throats. Terry cried out again and again. Then, suddenly, he was silent, and they could only see the bare walls of the empty and darkened flat. Terry was sitting down in the corner now, crying and muttering something. At first it was unintelligible, but soon they could make out what he was mumbling.

'I didn't do it, Mum. I didn't do it.'

He stared up at them blankly, then without warning his eyes began to focus again.

'You're safe after all, Tess,' he said, his voice much calmer, radiating relief.

'Yes,' said Sharon quietly. 'I'm safe after all.' Suddenly she was no longer frightened of him. Their roles seemed to have abruptly changed.

Eight

'Mrs Bonnington?'

'Has he given himself up?' she asked at once. Her face looked tired and drawn but there was a detachment to her that made Ian feel depressed.

'Not yet.'

She stood hopelessly in the doorway, looking as if she wanted them to go but didn't know how to say so. There was no sign of her husband at all. Ian stood his ground.

'I'd like to talk.'

'Who's this?' She cast a disapproving glance at Janata, as if he had come to tell her something she didn't want to hear.

'This is Mr Omfray. Janata Omfray. He is the male nurse who looked after Terry, who knew him best.'

'Well?' She still stood there impassively, barring their entrance.

'He'd like to talk to you.'

'To what end?' She spoke in a clipped, hostile way.

'To end this siege.' Ian let his feelings show and at last, startled by his anger, she stood back to let them in.

'Arthur!' she called.

'What is it now?' His voice came from somewhere at the back.

'People to see us.'

He came into the hall looking bleary and sleepy and Ian could hear the drone of the television. His anger stirred again. Why the hell weren't they trying to talk to their son? He could sense that Janata was feeling the same.

She led them into a front room that was over-furnished and scattered with so many holiday souvenirs that it looked like a bingo stand. Dolls from Holland and Spain, Portugal and France, Switzerland and Italy squatted on most surfaces and there were pictures made out of terracotta. The effect was dazzling, to say the least. Ian and Janata sat down gingerly on a garish chintz sofa while Arthur Bonnington plumped himself down in an armchair. His wife Anita sat disapprovingly on a hard upright chair. There was an ominous and prolonged silence.

'I told you before. There's nothing we can do for him. Nothing at all,' said Arthur at last and Anita shook her head in time with his words, as if verifying every single one of them.

'I'd like you to hear what Janata has to say,' said Ian crisply.

Arthur and Anita transferred their gaze to him as if he was some curious, hostile but rare species. Janata stuttered his way into speech, suddenly realising how very difficult it was going to be to convince them of anything. They were known to be totally prejudiced against their son and their attitude had obviously hardened over the years.

'I've known your son for some time,' he began.

'Oh, yes,' said Anita, as if he had asked her whether she'd enjoyed her dinner.

'Ever since he came to us.'

'Oh yes.' Anita continued with her zombie-like response while Arthur contented himself with a wooden stare.

'And I've becme very convinced that he didn't drown his sister.'

There was a cold and angry silence and Ian wished Janata had not come to the point so quickly. He was attacking them in their most vulnerable spot – and it showed.

'We *saw* him do it,' said Anita, her voice shaking.

'You don't know what you're talking about, young man,' said Arthur sharply. 'And besides, what the hell has all this got to do with what's going on up the road, eh? You can't come in here upsetting my wife like this. It's not right.' He looked indignantly at Ian. 'I'm very surprised you condone this intrusion, officer.'

'It's got everything to do with it,' rapped Ian. 'Give him a hearing.'

Mortally offended, they sat back and listened to Janata in a kind of martyred silence.

'You see, I honestly don't think he's capable of doing anything like that.'

'He's violent,' said Anita in a tiny, biting voice. 'Very violent indeed.'

'He gets very frustrated. He's mentally ill.'

'Is that all?' Arthur sneered.

80

'Yes, that *is* all. Terry has a lot of problems; a lot of reason to feel frustrated.'

'So you're claiming he's as sane as we are.'

Janata looked at their contorted faces and almost agreed. But he knew that if he was to help Terry then somehow he would have to get them on his side. And that seemed an increasingly impossible task.

'No. He's ill. But he could be helped.'

'How?'

'If he could feel that if he makes progress he can come home. That you will both visit him and encourage him to get better.'

'He killed his sister,' she repeated in a monotonous voice. 'How dare you speak to us like this.'

'That was never proven,' said Ian, suddenly deciding to back Janata all the way. If they could be shocked into action so much the better. 'Not if my reading of the case is correct.' It was true. He'd radioed for the background and they'd rushed him out a precis of the case.

'We know he killed her,' said Arthur. 'He drowned his own sister. Our little girl. The boy's a crazy psychopath and he'll kill again – mark my words. He was always a weirdo – even as a kid.'

With parents like you, no wonder, thought Ian bitterly. He felt sure they had always favoured the sister, always cast him out. Then he mentally shook himself. He was becoming as prejudiced as they were, just because they were so awful.

'He might kill if he was pushed,' said Janata significantly.

'What do you mean?' There was a flicker of unease in Arthur's eyes. Both Ian and Janata welcomed it.

'He might harm those kids. But he wouldn't if you helped him.'

'Helped him?' Anita's voice was frosty and indignant.

'If you would talk to him. Both of you.'

'There's no point,' began Arthur but Janata sensed that at last he had his wife's attention.

'Talk to him about what?' she asked. Ian thought she looked frightened. Maybe she reckoned she would be in trouble with the police if Terry did anything.

'If you could talk to him and say that you forgive him and you know that he didn't do it and you want him back home he'd be out of there like a shot,' said Janata, his words pouring out.

'No way,' said Arthur. 'You can't make us say all that cobblers.'

But Janata was warming to his sense of conviction. 'I know him. I really *know* him. Terry never stops talking about his home and is always wondering if he'll be forgiven. That's all he *ever* talks about.'

Ian watched Anita closely, for he knew that what Janata had said had touched on the vein of mother's love she still had for Terry despite all that had happened – all they suspected. But what *could* they have seen from the beach? he wondered. Surely they couldn't have seen much of what was actually going on.

Very hesitantly she said, 'I could try.'

It was like a miracle, Ian thought. Janata had managed to reach her, through layers of carefully constructed disassociation. Arthur however looked furious and Ian interposed quickly: 'You do have a duty to try and help those young people somehow. The longer your son holds them, the more chance there is of someone getting hurt.' He saw Arthur's anger replaced by reluctant acceptance and knew they had won this round at least.

'But we'd be lying,' said Anita. 'He can't come back here.'

'He's *never* coming back here,' Arthur shouted. 'But I suppose we'll have to.'

'Have to what?' asked Ian impatiently.

'Lie,' said Arthur.

Nine

'It's all right,' said Sharon. She sounded reassuring, affectionate, and Jonty watched her wide-eyed. 'It's all right.'

Terry was sitting on the floor, crying bitterly now.

'Come over and have a cuddle,' she continued.

He looked up at her like a wounded animal. 'They think I killed her.'

'And we know you didn't.'

'That doesn't help.'

'They *will* know,' said Sharon softly and warmly. 'They *will* know when I've finished with them.'

'Will *you* tell them, Tess?' Terry said with his now familiar double-think.

'Of course I will. Untie my arms and then I can give you a bit of a cuddle.'

'Is this a trick?' he asked, suddenly suspicious.

'No. What could I do against you? You're miles stronger than I am.'

Terry nodded and once again she noticed the strange split in his mind. On one level she was Tessa and on the other she was an enemy.

He came across and untied her arms. She stiffly rubbed them and then put them round him, pushing

84

herself away from Jonty as far as she could. She began to rock Terry to and fro like a baby.

'I didn't do it.'

'I know you didn't.'

'How will *they* know?'

Sharon thought at an amazing speed and suddenly came up with something that she had not thought of before. It would give Jonty a chance. But it was a slim one.

'They want a sign that you're a really responsible person.'

'Who wants a sign?'

'Your parents do, silly.'

'Don't you call me silly.'

He went rigid in her arms and Sharon knew that she had made a bad mistake. She stroked his hair and whispered, 'Sorry.'

'No one calls me silly.'

'I won't ever again.'

'Cross your heart and hope to die.'

'Cross my heart and hope to die.'

'What were you on about?'

'You can let him go.'

'Who?'

'Let Jonty go.'

'Him?' He looked across at Jonty doubtfully.

'Yes, him.' Sharon forced herself to sound calm and natural.

'Why?'

'Because it would look as though you cared for someone.'

'I care for *you*, Tess.'

'I know you do.' She stroked his hair again, surprised that she was not finding holding and stroking him a horrible experience. 'But you see there's a lot of people outside worrying about him, and I expect your parents are coming soon, and I know they'll want you to treat everyone very kindly.'

'And if they see me being kind, will they let me go home?'

For a moment she did not want to lie to him; a split second later she knew that she would have to for all their sakes.

'Of course they'll want you to go home.'

'And you'll be with me, won't you, Tess? You'll come home with me and then Mum and Dad will be ever so pleased.'

'Of course I'll come with you.'

'Promise?'

'I promise.'

He looked at Jonty again. 'We never wanted him on our holiday in the first place.'

'No,' said Sharon. 'We never did.'

'And if I send him home it'll be just the two of us.'

'That's right.'

'No one else will come, will they?'

'No.'

Terry got up and went over to Jonty. He began to untie him, but Jonty said quietly, 'I won't go without you, Sharon.'

'You must.'

Terry went on untying him as if he hadn't heard, but Jonty was determined.

'I'm staying with you.'

'You're not,' she said sharply. 'You *must* go.'

'Yeah. You hop off, son. We don't want you.'

'I'm *not going*.'

'You *are*,' yelled Sharon and Terry together.

'You mean that's what you were on about; you *want* us to lie to him?' asked Anita. She still looked very indecisive.

'No,' said Janata.

'Yes,' said Ian.

Janata turned on him furiously but Ian decided his only chance was to side with the wavering Bonningtons. 'Don't be naive, son,' he said in his most stolid manner. 'We have to get them out at any cost.'

'But if he's lied to now he'll never trust anyone again.'

'We *have* to get them out. Away from him. Don't you understand?'

Janata did and he nodded miserably. 'There's no love for Terry at all here,' he said to Arthur sadly.

'Not after what he did. He's a nutter and that's all there is to it. We want to forget him.'

Janata turned to Anita. 'And you?'

'Don't you cross-examine my wife. A raw kid like you,' began Arthur aggressively, but to everyone's surprise Anita interrupted him.

'Yes, I do love him still. He's my child and I still love that child. But I can't reconcile myself to what Terry has become – or what he's done. I'm prepared to help out now and lie to him, if that's the only way we can help those poor kids he has locked up with him. Is that right?'

87

Ian nodded. 'That's right, Mrs Bonnington,' he said, trying not to notice Janata's accusing eyes boring into him. 'Now let's run over what we're going to do.'

Everyone was taken off their guard when Jonty reluctantly staggered out of the flat and into the arms of the waiting police. Ian had not yet arrived back from the Bonningtons' so it was the community policeman Reg who was the first to talk to him. Jonty was stiff, and his wrists and ankles were raw where he had been tied up; otherwise he was unhurt. But he was deeply upset that he had been forced to leave Sharon, and he wept bitterly as he told Reg all about it.

'They made me come out,' he kept repeating, between sobs.

'Both of them?'

'They said I *had* to come. It wasn't fair.'

'I thought you'd be pleased to be released, son.'

'And leave her with that Terry? He's barmy.'

'Hang on.' Mr Bonnington was just about to get to his feet when he looked at Janata and had second thoughts. 'I thought I recognised you. Didn't I see you with that Imran – the kid whose old man owns the supermarket?'

'Probably.'

'Then aren't you the coloured bloke who's got AIDS?' Mrs Bonnington leapt to her feet as her husband continued: 'The coloured bloke who's moving in on this estate? I heard all about it from some young blokes who were hanging round the square.'

Janata started. He had no idea that people would have started talking about him so quickly and he felt desperately exposed. Ian intervened quickly.

'Look, we've got no time to talk. There's a siege going on.'

But Arthur was not to be deterred. 'And you're my son's nurse?'

'What is all this?' Anita asked wide-eyed. 'I don't want to get mixed up in any more trouble.'

'I've got HIV.'

'What's that when it's at home?' Arthur asked truculantly.

'It's a virus.'

'It's the beginning,' Anita said dramatically. 'It's the beginning of all that AIDS stuff. I read it in the papers and they're always talking about it on telly.'

'You queer, then?' asked Arthur aggressively.

Janata turned away, the angry tears stinging in his eyes, and Ian rushed in again, trying to stem the tide of the Bonningtons' anger and fear.

'Drop it,' he said. 'This is totally irrelevant. We have to get back to Terry. Anything could be happening.'

'I'm not having nothing to do with *him*,' said Arthur. 'Bloody queer looking after my Terry.'

'So he's *your* Terry, is he?' blazed Ian, unable to control himself any longer. 'When did you become so fond of him? I thought you'd disowned him.'

'I'm not having it. It's not right, him being looked after by a queer with AIDS.'

'Will you *shut up*?'

Janata still had his back to them and felt he

couldn't turn round. Ian came up and put his arm round his shoulders, glaring at Anita who had winced.

'This man has come forward to help handle your son and we're damn lucky that he's taken the trouble to volunteer. Now, stop insulting him and let's get going.'

'Well, really,' said Anita. 'I asure you that I'm not used to being spoken to like this, especially by a policeman.'

Ian ignored her, pushing Janata towards the door. They followed, disapproval and affront oozing from their compressed lips. 'Do everything you can to calm your son down and get him out of that flat,' said Ian authoritatively.

They mumbled something, but whether it was to do with the lies they were going to tell Terry or the prejudice they held for Janata was not clear. Ian put his arm round Janata's shoulder again and said softly, 'You're doing a great job, Janata.'

'Feeling better?' asked Sharon.

'Yes,' replied Terry sulkily.

'Want a cup of tea?'

'I'll get it.'

'If you untie my feet, I could get it for you.'

'Yes, and you might do a runner on me.'

'How could I?'

'You'd take your chance.'

She lay there, her feet numb, while he went to put some water in the kettle. It was late afternoon, she supposed, and there had been no sound from outside for ages.

'Thanks for letting Jonty go.'

'I never wanted him. Not on *our* holiday.'

'What are we going to do next?'

'I'm going to take you home. The holiday's over now.'

A surge of relief went through Sharon. Did it mean that he was going to let her go? Then her hopes were swiftly dashed. Terry began to talk again, but this time she found his words dead and leaden. There was no magic any more.

'Here we go, just walking down to the flat. Do you know that when I ran away from the hospital once I saw a copper sitting with my mum and dad? That's because they were scared of me. Fancy being scared of me. Are you scared of me?'

'Of course I'm not,' said Sharon as convincingly as she could.

'I mean, you wouldn't be scared of your own brother, would you?' He poured out the tea and brought her a cup.

Sharon said nothing, wondering what he was going to do next.

'Here we are. I don't know what they're going to think. Anyway, they're in for a big surprise, aren't they? I mean they really are. They thought that you were dead and instead of all that I've brought you home safe and sound. Hallo, Mum. Hallo, Dad. I'm knocking on the door and shouting through the letter box and I'm going to give them a big surprise, aren't I?' he said, looking at her for reassurance.

91

'You certainly are,' she replied quickly.

'Here they are opening up the door, and I've got you and they're pleased.' He paused. He was standing in the middle of the room quite still and staring at the wall. His eyes were wide and unblinking. 'Mum. Dad. I've brought her back. Aren't you pleased? Isn't this a surprise? Are you thrilled? She never drowned. All that happened was that I rescued her and she was safe and sound. We were swimming out to the island, and we were safe. She got a bit frightened – well, that's certainly true. She got a bit frightened and all that and I said – well, it doesn't matter what I said, but when you looked from the beach – it was all right. It was all right, Mum. Honest, it was all right, Dad. What do you mean?' His voice rose higher and higher in a terrible kind of despair. 'What do you mean?'

'What's the matter, Terry?' Sharon was worried. He seemed to be cracking up completely now.

'What do you mean?' He was screaming the phrase into thin air and she couldn't reach him. He was somewhere else. He turned to stare at her and she saw something in his eyes that really terrified her. He was looking at her differently, as if he had recognised her for the first time.

Then Terry turned back to the wall and began to shout again. 'What do you mean I've brought home the wrong girl? Of course she's not the wrong girl. This is Tess. My sister Tess. It's not?' He looked stunned, as if the revelation might kill him, but he also looked as if he believed in what he was being told in his mind and he stared at Sharon with dawning

92

comprehension. 'That's right, Dad. I've made a mistake. I'm sorry. This isn't Tess. This isn't Tess. But I never hurt her. She'll turn up, you'll see. It wasn't like you saw from the beach. Not like that at all. Honest, Dad. Don't hurt me, Dad. I don't know who this girl is – pretending to be Tessa.'

He turned back to Sharon and spat at her. The spittle ran down her face and she was too afraid to wipe it away. Her whole body was shaking; she knew that Terry's nightmare had deepened and that there was no further help that she could possibly give him.

Ten

Ian was delighted to find that Jonty had been released. He seemed physically fine, but was very distressed and stood with his mother while Ian spoke to him gently. Imran, Mick, Gallica, Janata and the Bonningtons had also joined them behind the screen that had been placed between those involved in the siege and the gathering crowd and television cameramen that were lining up on the other side, eagerly waiting for news. They could dimly hear one news reporter talking on mike. 'There has been a new development in the Starling Point siege when one of the hostages, a deaf boy of fifteen, was released half an hour ago. Now that the . . . '

'You really OK, Jonty?' asked Ian again, deeply relieved that at least one of the children had been released.

'He didn't hurt me much. But she's in there. You have to get her out.'

'We're going to do everything we can, I assure you of that. But can you tell me what kind of relationship Sharon has made with Terry? If any?'

'It's good.'

'Thank God.'

'She's helping him. Trying to help him. But he's all mixed-up.'

'And he hasn't hurt her?'

'No. He took us on holiday.'

'What?'

'Like with his voice. He must be a genius. It felt as if we were there. It was amazing.'

'What did he say?'

'He talked us down to Cornwall. We went on the beach and for a swim and then something happened to his sister. But he thinks Sharon *is* his sister. And he said that something happened but he rescued her. It was amazing,' said Jonty again. 'You could taste the sea.'

Ian turned to Janata and asked him what he thought.

'Terry often relives that experience. Most days of his life, in fact.' Janata was obviously trying to speak calmly but they could all see that he was very worried indeed.

'What's the matter?' said Ian sharply.

'Terry has a certain behaviour pattern and it goes through phases. He relives the drowning and then imagines that he's saved Tessa and is bringing her home to his parents and they will realise that it was all a misunderstanding and forgive him and he will return to a happy home.'

'And then?'

'But when he actually gets there he realises he's brought the wrong girl home. It's like a perpetual waking nightmare that brings him continually from elation to despair, and so far the cycle has never been broken. He's had a lot of treatment but it's never broken the cycle.'

'What do you mean?'

'Well, while Terry imagines he's rescued Tess he's safe and loving – if very domineering. But once he moves into the rejection part – when he realises he's brought home the wrong girl and his parents are even angrier with him than ever – then he becomes really dangerous.' Janata paused. 'I'm very sorry I didn't say all this before but I never thought that Terry would involve real people in the cycle. In the hospital it was always just in his mind.'

'How dangerous is he in a rage?' asked Ian.

'He has to be strapped down.'

'You mean in a straitjacket?'

'Yes.'

'Will his parents be as useful as we'd hoped?'

'They could be.'

'Could they make him worse?'

'They'll have to take a very loving, forgiving atti-tude to him – if they are capable of it,' said Janata in a low voice.

'I think they should go into action immediately,' said Ian.

'You're not my sister.'

'I never said I was, Terry.'

He was towering over her. 'You *said* you were my sister.'

'*You* said I was.'

'You've been lying to me.'

'I've been trying to help you.'

'No.'

'Yes I have, Terry. And I want to go *on* helping you.'

'You have to be punished.'

'Why?'

'You said you were my sister when you weren't.'

'Terry, I want to *help* you.'

'No.'

'What about your parents? They wouldn't want you to hurt me. Don't you want them to forgive you?'

'I don't care what they do now.'

'Why?'

'I can't find Tess. They'll never forgive me if I can't find Tess.'

'I could help you.'

'How? Do you know where she is?' Instantly he was suspicious.

'We could talk about it. Try to work it out.'

'You *tell* me where she is.'

'Let's take it slowly. We've got to think about it carefully.'

His rage was beginning to boil over. Terry threw the remains of his now cold tea in her face. 'If you don't tell me now I'll kill you,' he shouted.

'I can't take much more of this,' said Imran. He looked at his watch and saw that it was almost seven in the evening.

Mick grinned miserably. 'How do you think I feel?'

'Sorry.'

97

'It's OK. But we just can't stand here for ever. I want some action.'

'I think they're going to get his parents to talk to him.'

'Let's hope that'll do some good,' said Mick. 'If not I think they should rush him. I would.'

Gallica looked at him in concern. 'For God's sake,' she hissed. 'Don't do anything stupid.'

'Take the megaphone and speak slowly and distinctly into it. When he comes out, speak to him without it.' Ian gave the instructions to Anita first as he knew that Arthur could ruin everything for them just by the tone of his voice.

'I can't cope with this thing,' she whispered, holding the megaphone away from her.

'You must try,' he said firmly, and although Arthur started to say something vitriolic Ian cut him short by picking up the megaphone and calling, 'Terry. Terry Bonnington.' He kept repeating his name but for the first few minutes there was no reply at all. Then, to everyone's mixed alarm and relief, Terry came to the window.

'Push off,' he said.

'I have your mother for you.'

There was a long pause and then Terry said something that Ian and Janata had so dreaded to hear.

'It's too late,' he said. 'I don't want to speak to them.'

'Nothing's too late, Terry,' said Ian persistently.

'She *wasn't* my sister.'

'She's a girl called Sharon. You musn't hurt her.'

98

Terry said nothing and Mick grabbed Imran's arm as he moved instinctively forward.

'Don't blow it now or we're finished.'

'That's rich coming from you,' said Imran, but he stopped moving.

'How *is* Sharon, Terry?' asked Ian.

Again there was no reply.

'I'm going to ask your mother to speak to you.'

Still no reply. Anita raised the megaphone to her trembling lips.

'Terry.'

No reply.

'Terry. I want to come closer and talk to you and not have to use this silly thing. Is that all right?'

Still no answer. Trembling even more, Anita put the megaphone down and moved forward. Surprised that she was coping at all, Ian began to walk with her towards the flat window, but immediately Terry yelled, 'You come alone, Mum.'

Ian paused and she went on alone.

'Hallo, son,' she said quietly. 'What are you doing in there?'

'That girl. She said she was Tess.'

'I want you to come out of there, son.'

'I'm not going back to the hospital.'

'Why not come home for tea?'

'You're lying, Mum.' Suddenly his voice was quite normal and Ian and all the others, straining their ears to catch his words, recognised a new, more destructive phase. He wasn't a child to be duped. He knew she was lying; instinctively he had it all worked out.

'I'm not lying. Why should I lie to you?' Even more surprisingly, Anita seemed calmer by the moment.

'Because the copper told you to, Mum. And because Dad told you to as well.'

'He wants you to come home.'

'He wants me to come out. So they can get me.'

'No one will get you.'

'Dad wouldn't want me home. Not ever.'

'Would you like him to come and talk to you?'

'He'd be lying, too.'

'We want you back with us, Terry.'

'If you'd wanted me, Mum, then you wouldn't have let them put me in that hospital.'

'It was best for you. You needed help.' Still she was calm.

'I needed *you*. I needed you to *believe* me.'

'I'm sorry.'

'You still think that I killed her, don't you?'

'No.'

'You do, and he does as well. You think I killed Tess.'

'It was an accident.'

'You think I drowned her.'

'No.'

'Go away, Mum.'

'What are you going to do?'

'You punished me for something I didn't do, so I'm going to punish this girl. This girl Sharon. Now go away.'

'Terry – '

'Go to hell, Mum. Go to hell.'

Anita broke down crying and hurried back to the

police line, but as she did so there was a roar of rage and Mick broke from the crowd, yelling and screaming at Terry. Imran began to run after him. For a while it looked as if no one else was going to move, then, too late, three policemen joined in the chase. It was Imran who brought Mick down and held him yelling and struggling on the ground, bellowing out Sharon's name over and over again while Gallica tried her best to calm him.

Terry came back into the kitchen. Sharon had heard nothing of what was going on beyond his continuous shouting. But when he faced her she knew that she was in terrible danger. He stood over her, clenching and unclenching his fists, his eyes blank, not seeing her, and there was a little bit of foam coming out of his mouth. She had to keep calm, Sharon kept telling herself. It was her only hope. She must remain as calm and as soothing as she could. Please God help me, she prayed. Please God help me. She closed her eyes and could just hear Terry's breathing, which was very short and sharp. Soon he started muttering to himself, but this time she was quite unable to make out what he was saying.

'If you can't control yourself, Michael, I'm going to ask you to go and wait behind the screen.'

'You can't do that.'

'I can and I will. Please. We're doing our best. Don't sabotage it now.'

Mick was sitting on the ground with a couple of policemen either side of him.

'What's happening?'

Mick looked up and groaned. It was his mum and dad. They had been out all day but now they had arrived, hot and flustered and full of anxious questions. The policeman who had waited at the flat for them was obviously trying to explain, but they weren't listening.

'Mr and Mrs Newby?' asked Ian.

'That's us,' said Mr Newby. 'What's going on? Where's Sharon?'

'Your daughter is in that flat being held hostage by a mental patient.' He brought out the crisp and horrifying little explanation as quickly as he could.

The Newbys looked totally bewildered at first but then the full horror of the situation began to seep through to them.

'My God!' shrieked Mrs Newby.

'We're trying to keep this area as quiet and as calm as we can, so we'd be grateful if you would keep to that rule. We don't want to alarm the young man concerned in any way.'

Mick expected his father to bluster but he stood his ground, staring at the half-open window of the flat and putting his arm round his wife who was convulsed with spasms of silent sobbing. They looked broken and pathetic, and for the first time in years Mick was moved by the way they so suddenly needed each other. It takes something like this to bring it out of them, he thought cynically.

'Would you please go and join Terry's parents the other side of the screen?' asked Ian. 'You'll be kept fully informed of everything that happens, and I can assure you that we are doing all we can to bring this situation to an end.' He knew that he sounded horribly officious.

'What action are you taking?' asked Mr Newby.

'We're talking him down.'

'I don't see much evidence of that.'

'He's thinking things over.'

'And what's Mick doing sitting with those policemen?'

'He got a little upset. But he's fine now, aren't you, Michael?'

'I'm fine, Dad.' His voice was expressionless.

'Why are you letting these kids in and not us?' He looked angrily at his own son and Imran, his gaze eventually resting on Gallica.

'We hoped the presence of Sharon's brother and boyfriend might help, but it hasn't so far. They'll probably be joining you behind the screen any moment.'

Mr Newby looked doubtfully at him and then led his still silently sobbing wife away without uttering another word. For the first time in his life Mick felt something for his father: pride. He had conducted himself well.

'Terry.'

'You shut up.'

'I want to help you.'

'You. You started all this. I'm going to punish you.'

Please God, she prayed inwardly. Please God, help me. Do something. Stop him. Don't let him hurt me.

Out loud she went on reasoning with him, although she was conscious that she now sounded hopelessly afraid. Perhaps it doesn't matter, she thought. Perhaps it will make him feel *some* compassion. 'Please don't hurt me,' she pleaded.

Terry looked at her for the first time since he had come back from speaking to his mother, and to her horror she saw that his eyes and whole face were completely devoid of any expression at all. He was totally self-absorbed; the outward part of him had turned inward. It was horrible to see.

'You should be punished.'

'You kidnapped me from the street. It's not my fault.'

'You said you were my sister.'

'No. *You* said it,' she replied wearily.

Terry came closer to her and Sharon closed her eyes, waiting for him to hit her. Then she heard him walking away and coming back again. What had he gone to fetch? Something to hurt her with? She forced herself to open her eyes and saw that he was standing over her with a box of matches. This time he was grinning.

Eleven

'Terry.' Ian was back on the megaphone and Imran could feel the tension tightening an extra notch in all of them.

'Terry.'

There was no sign of him.

'Terry,' he called again and again and after some time Terry reluctantly reappeared. He looked vague and distracted and answered in a monotonous, matter-of-fact sort of voice.

'What do you want?'

'Terry. I have your dad to speak to you.'

'I don't want to listen to him.'

'Give him a try.'

Impatiently Arthur Bonnington took the megaphone and said: 'Terry.'

'What do you want, Dad?' Terry's voice was still dull and uninterested.

'I want you home. Home with us.'

'For ever?'

'You bet.' Arthur sounded convincing and there was a warmth in his voice that Ian would not have believed possible. He was a good actor was Arthur.

'You're lying, Dad.' Terry's voice was very positive and everyone's hopes plummeted again.

'Listen, Terry. Why should I lie to you? Why should your dad lie to you?' Arthur was still calm.

'Because you want me to come out.'

The answer was so rational that Imran gave an involuntary groan of despair and the two policemen moved a little nearer Mick. There were tears running down Mick's face and his whole body was taut with rage.

'Of course I want you to come out. I want you at home, safe and sound.'

'You know what? You're a liar, Dad.'

'Look, Terry, just one thing.'

'What?'

'Take a risk. Trust me.'

'No way. All that's going to happen is that the filth are going to jump me and take me back to that hospital or worse.'

'No.'

'That's what's going to happen, Dad. Now go away.'

'What about the girl?' Ian asked Terry as he took the megaphone away from Arthur, who for the first time looked genuinely afraid.

'She's being punished.'

The two policemen immediately took hold of Mick who began to struggle desperately. One of them put his hand over Mick's mouth as he bellowed obscenities at Terry.

'Let me talk to him, Ian.' Imran couldn't bear his own inaction any longer. 'Please, I won't blow it.'

Ian silently handed him the megaphone.

'Terry.'

'Who wants me?'

'That girl Sharon.'

'What about her?'

'She's my girlfriend.'

'She's being punished.' Terry's voice was childishly stubborn.

'*Please* don't hurt her.'

'She deserves it.'

'She's a very special person to me. Like Tess was to you.'

'Why should I care what *you* feel?'

'I love her.' Imran's voice broke, but Terry was impervious.

'That's nothing to do with me.'

'Look – '

'I'm going in again.'

'One thing.'

'Yeah?'

'Suppose you take me. And let her go?'

Terry laughed as if he had just heard a very good joke. 'You must think I'm potty,' he said and disappeared.

'We'll have to rush him,' muttered Ian, and Mick looked up with sudden hope in his eyes. Action was the one thing he understood; the inaction had been intolerable to him.

'Wait a minute.' It was Janata. 'Can *I* speak to him?'

'Why?' asked Imran.

'Hang on,' said Ian. 'What would you say? I reckon everything's been said.'

'This might be our last chance. Let me have a few seconds. Please.'

With sudden decision Ian handed him the megaphone. He wanted to try everything before he had to send in the squad of special policemen who specialised in breaking sieges and who were waiting behind the screen. He felt he had failed. Usually he managed to talk down what he had come to term his 'clients'. But not this time.

'Terry.'

He came out again condescendingly, glad to have so much attention, but getting impatient with the repetitious comments.

'Do you recognise my voice?'

Terry paused. 'No.'

'It's Janata.'

Terry paused again. 'What the hell do you want?'

'To talk.'

'No, I've talked too much.'

'We've always been able to talk, Terry.'

'So – '

'I can't talk through this thing.'

'Come closer.' Terry laughed good-naturedly. 'I won't bite you.'

'I want to talk to you inside.'

'Why?'

'So we can really talk. Relaxed like.'

'It's a trick – another trick.'

'I'm coming alone.'

'You'll bring something.'

'What do you mean?'

'A gun or something.' Terry suddenly sounded childish.

'I don't know anything about guns.'

'Something else then. Something to hurt me with.'

'You can search me. I just want to talk.'

'What have you got to say?'

Janata paused. He knew that he had to have something to offer. But what? He had nothing. Then he took a risk by saying the first thing that came into his head. 'I know where Tess is.'

'Don't give me that garbage.'

'She did drown, Terry. But she's in her grave. I could take you there.'

'I don't want to see her grave.'

'And I could prove to everyone that you didn't kill her.' He was lying now, but Janata knew that he had to get in somehow; by any method, whatever the risk to himself. Suddenly Terry was his own personal responsibility.

'How?' Terry sounded only vaguely interested.

'I've got proof.'

'What is it?'

'Someone took a photograph. A photograph from the shore. It proves that you were trying to save her.'

There was a short silence.

'Liar.'

'I've got it here.'

'Bring it.'

'If I can see you inside the flat.'

'Show it to me first.'

'Inside.'

'This is a trick.'

'You'll have to take a risk.'

'Come on, then,' said Terry with sudden decision. 'And if you're lying I'll punish you. Like I'm punishing her.'

'OK.'

'Obviously I can't let you do this,' said Ian emphatically as Janata passed him back the megaphone.

'Please.'

'No.'

'I *can* talk him down. I have many times in the past.'

'Not in a situation like this.'

'I've been alone with him when he's been really raving. And I talked him down then. I can do it again.'

'We'll rush him. I've got a special squad. The time for talking's finished.'

'*Please* let me try.'

'Do you have this photograph?'

'Of course not.'

'Are you crazy?'

'I tell you I can talk to him.'

'He could kill you.'

'He won't.'

'What about the photograph? It's the first thing he'll ask for.'

'If I can get in I'll be OK. And I reckon I can. Please let me try.'

'We'll let you go – and then rush him.'

'No.' Janata was emphatic now. 'If he suspects a

trick, he'll go mad and kill us both. Let me just try this way.'

Ian hesitated. Then he said: 'We'll give you half an hour. But if he attacks you or her, shout and we'll be there in a few seconds.'

Janata nodded. 'It's all I need. I want to take the chance.'

'Good on you,' said Mick and Imran said he would pray for him. Gallica watched miserably; she was sure the siege had all the potential now to end in tragedy.

'I'll need those prayers,' said Janata as he set off towards the window – and Terry. He did not have any of the confidence that he had shown to the others. But he was determined to try.

Terry was sweating despite the cool of the evening. It was getting dark now and Janata couldn't see into the shadowed interior of the derelict flat, but he could smell a sharp, musty smell and Janata instinctively knew that it was the smell of fear.

'I haven't got it,' said Janata pausing.

'Eh?'

'I haven't got the photograph. It was a lie to get near you. I'm sorry I raised your hopes.' Janata had one hand on the windowsill and he reached out the other for Terry. 'Help me in.'

'Everyone lies to me,' said Terry, ignoring the hand.

'They're afraid of you. But Sharon didn't lie to you. It was you that lied to her.'

'How do you make that out?'

'The facts.'

'I don't want to see you. You can go to hell.'

'Terry – do you want to go back to that hospital?'

'I'm never going back there. It's a prison.'

'Supposing you went somewhere else?'

'I want to go home,' he wailed childishly and Janata felt a spark of hope.

'We can't talk over a windowsill. Let me in and we can talk properly. Search me if you want. I don't have any weapon unless you count a biro, and I wouldn't have the guts to use anything anyway.'

Terry was silent. Then he said: 'What is there to talk about?'

Janata was familiar with this mood. It was the calm before the storm; the riskiest possible moment to deal with Terry, for he was often very calm before he went into one of his manic rages. Janata knew he had to survive the first half of the storm and then wait for the eye – the still, calm centre when Terry would dissolve into dependent tears. The major drawback was that Janata had no help and he was in a derelict flat and not the familiar surroundings of the hospital. But he had no choice; he had to see it through. He was also aware that his time was limited.

'There's a lot to talk about.'

'You lied to me.'

'I told you why.'

Terry was silent again and there was a long pause.

'Are you going to lie to me again?'

'No.'

'What do you want?'

'The police have given me half an hour and it's ticking away fast.'

'What then?'

'They'll rush you.'

'I'll kill her.'

'And you'll spend the rest of your life inside.'

'So what can *you* do?' Terry scoffed.

'There's a place I know.'

'Another prison.'

'No. It's by the sea.'

'Why can't I go home?'

'You know the answer to that.'

'So they *were* lying to me?'

'It was the only way they had. They're just as frightened as the rest of us.'

'So you're all frightened of me?'

'Of course we are.'

Terry smiled. The idea seemed to afford him a good deal of pleasure, and Janata thanked God that he had hit on the right note. The calm was still there, although he knew that the storm was not far away.

Ian was talking to the squad of special policemen. They were armed, wore helmets and protective clothing and carried shields. They had been placed the other side of the screen where Terry couldn't see them. The problem was that the parents could, and the Newbys were being comforted by members of the crowd.

'What entrances are there?' asked Sergeant Bentley who was in charge of the squad.

'Nothing much,' replied Ian brusquely. 'There's the

front, as you've seen it, and at the back there's a very narrow kitchen window.'

'And from above?'

'Another empty flat and I've got men there. But there's a concrete floor between the two.'

'And the siege is taking place in the kitchen?'

'Yes. It's the front or nothing.'

'It's not good. He could do a lot of damage while we're getting in. Are you going to give this nurse bloke any more time?'

Ian looked at his watch. 'He's got seven minutes left.'

'And then we go in?'

'Then we go in.'

Twelve

'I'm Sharon's mother.'

'I'm Terry's mother.'

The two men stood glowering at each other, but the two women had been drawn together and they stood by the screen trying to see round it and trying not to look at the armed police with their riot shields and helmets.

'I'm very sorry,' said Anita humbly.

But Mrs Newby wanted to meet her halfway. More than anything she wanted the comfort of another woman, for although she had turned to her husband at first she was finding there was so little between them that he couldn't give her the support and understanding she so badly needed.

'You can't help having a handicapped child. I know someone else on the estate who's got one with Down's Syndrome. And then there's Jonty. You know, the deaf one your son was holding.'

The men listened silently, as if a miracle was taking place. The women who had been beside themselves with anguish were now almost talking normally, while the riot squad prepared to go in and spotlights were being turned on to the front of the flat. The television crew were still hovering, hungry for action, and there were any amount of photographers. But somehow the two women were holding each other together with sympathy and an understanding that surpassed their fears and the horrors of the present situation.

'They're not like Terry.'

'Well, he can't help it, can he?'

'I thought you would all be calling him a monster.'

'He's your son, isn't he? You know how desperately afraid for Sharon I am, but I can't hold you responsible for having him, can I?'

'We went wrong. Tess was our favourite and we showed it.'

'Well, we've done the same thing with my son. He went off the rails last year and that was because we favoured Sharon. Now it's too late to put it right, although I do try. But he's a very difficult boy, and although he's doing better now he's still not easy. He's picked up with this African girl. And you know my Sharon goes out with a Pakistani. Not that he's not a nice boy, mark you, but who would have though it'd come to that? Of course they've all moved into Starling Point. They call it a melting pot. Now, when I was a girl – '

The other woman listened eagerly, hoping for and receiving distraction from what was happening, and they settled down to a long talk that was half prejudiced and half loving. The two men continued to listen in amazement.

'Blimey. Typical women,' said Arthur at last.

'You'd have thought they were talking over the fence.'

'If it keeps them from worrying.'

'Terry's a nutter, you see.'

'Oh yes?'

And the two men also began to talk.

'You OK?'

Grubby and very white and frightened, she was lying on the floor with her legs tied, but thankfully she didn't look as if she had been harmed. Sharon stared up at Janata in amazement, and he could see the painful hope in her eyes.

'I work with Terry at the hospital. I'm a nurse and I've come to talk things over with him.'

'Nothing to talk about,' said Terry. He picked up the box of matches.

'What are you doing with those, Terry?'

'Little boy mustn't play with matches?' he mocked. He struck one and waved it under Sharon's nose and then blew it out. She recoiled in terror.

'Listen, Terry, we don't have much time,' said Janata, injecting as much urgency into his voice as possible.

'I'm listening.'

'Give yourself up and let her go unharmed and everything will be so much better for you.'

'It couldn't be worse. I'll be inside for the rest of my natural. What have I got to lose?'

'A lot.'

'What?' He laughed but there was a trace of uneasiness there and Janata seized on it quickly.

'You could be inside for the rest of your life and it could be a very nasty place indeed. But if you give up peacefully we could work out this place you could go to by the sea. You could learn a trade and –'

'How long would I be there?'

'Till you're better.'

'That's what they said at the hospital, but they never said when I could get out. That's why I did this bunk. Right?'

'You might like the place I'm talking about.' Janata was very conscious of how naïve he must be sounding and how very little he had to offer Terry. He was also horribly aware that Terry knew this and was scoffing at him.

'How could *you* get me there? A nurse? You don't have any power.'

'My opinion is asked.'

'Yeah.'

'And particularly now that I've come in here.'

'They'll just think you're a mug.'

'I can try.'

'That's not good enough.' Terry lit another match and held it over Sharon and then blew it out. He laughed gently.

'Wherever you go,' said Sharon unexpectedly, 'I'll come and visit you, Terry.'

'I don't want to see you. You don't mean it, anyway.'

Sharon suddenly lost her temper, the hours of rigid self-control were finally beginning to tell on her. 'Don't you call me a liar,' she shouted. 'You kidnapped me, you bastard, and I never told you anything but my real name, and I've even offered to visit you and you don't care. You're a bastard, Terry.'

He stared at her as if she had hit him, and then, gibbering with rage, lit another match. Janata recognised that the calm was over. Terry began to yell and scream like an angry child. Janata tried to talk him down as he did at the hospital, but he had no back up and therefore knew that he had no chance.

'You don't have to guard me now,' said Mick. He spoke very clearly and quietly. 'I'm not going anywhere. In fact, I'm going behind the screen. I can't stand watching this any more.'

'Very sensible of you, son,' said one of the policemen. 'It'll soon be over and they'll get your sister out. We've got the heavy squad going in in a minute.'

'Great.' Mick stood up and the policemen stood up with him, still suspicious but giving way a little. 'You coming?' Mick said to Imran and winked quickly, taking care he had his back to the policemen.

'I'm coming,' said Imran.

Gallica saw the wink but she felt rooted to the spot. Events were out of control, and she couldn't think what to do or who to stop.

Terry struck another match and this time threw it at Sharon. It fizzled out but it was still terrifying. She screamed as he lit another, but this time he picked up a newspaper and turned it into a flaming torch. Looking round, Janata saw that there was a pile of old newspapers by the kitchen door. He stole a glance at his watch. He had five minutes left. Maybe five minutes too long. If Terry lit the other papers they could have a real blaze and maybe that was what he wanted.

'Terry – '

'You shut up.'

'What are you doing?'

'I don't want to go anywhere. I'm not going anywhere. Get it?'

'No.'

'I'm going to start a fire. Yes, that's what I'm going to do.' He laughed and hurled the fiercely burning newspaper into the corner where it caught the others. 'We're going to have a fire. A good fire.' He turned to Sharon. 'And I'm not going to help you, Tess. You shouldn't have swum back to the beach. I told you you wouldn't make it. People don't listen to me. They have to listen to me. It's not fair if they don't. But you didn't, so you have to be punished like Dad punished me. He used to beat me, Tess. Mum never stopped him. No one wants me, Tess. Not even you. Because you swam away.'

Smoke from the papers began to invade the room and Terry lit yet another match.

'Right,' said Mick. 'Coming?' He began to run towards the flats, followed by Imran and Gallica.

'Stop!' yelled one of the policemen, giving chase, but all three were too quick for them and they were up to the flat and over the windowsill before anyone could stop them.

'No, Terry.'

'Why not?'

'Think what you'll be doing.'

'I don't care what I do.' He began to rave and shout and Janata knew that he was coming to the peak of his tantrum and there would not be enough time to wait for the calm period – the eye of the storm.

'Please, Terry,' said Sharon quietly, her temper gone. 'I'll come and see you.'

'No one's coming to see anyone,' he yelled and struck more matches, hurling them at the already blazing heap. An old chair had caught now and was giving off acrid fumes that were already making Sharon choke. There was only one thing for it. Janata threw himself at Terry's vast bulk and, taken by surprise, he collapsed on the floor with Janata on top of him.

'There's smoke,' yelled Gallica.

'Go on,' said Imran as they scrambled inside. 'Don't stop. We'll rush him together.'

'Send in the squad,' said Ian, cursing the speed of the two boys and Gallica. This had been the most disastrous siege he had ever been involved in and he feared for its outcome. In a few seconds the police squad had run from behind the barrier and were heading for the window, riot shields up. When they got there they put the shields down on the ground and got out their weapons. Covering each other they began to penetrate the flat with Ian hard on their heels.

Terry rolled Janata off him in a matter of moments and pulled him to his feet. They were both coughing and Sharon felt completely choked by the dense smoke that was now filling the kitchen. The flames that were spreading from the corner crackled fiercely, but the proximity of death did not make her cry out; instead she watched Terry begin to hit Janata without saying a word. She crouched there, terrified, not knowing what to do but convinced that this was going to be the end of them all.

Suddenly, miraculously, she heard shouting from the other room and Mick, Imran and Gallica burst in. Imran and Gallica came straight for her, choking and gasping in the smoke, while Mick threw himself at Terry. The smoke was now so dense that it was getting difficult to see clearly; Mick swung at Terry and completely missed. But Terry was totally absorbed in hitting Janata in the face as hard and as many times as he could. Sharon could just make out that he was bleeding heavily as she choked and choked again and Imran and Gallica struggled frantically with her bonds.

Eventually there was a loud thud as Mick managed to hit Terry at last and he swung away from Janata with a howl of rage and flung himself on Mick. Instantly Imran left Gallica to untie Sharon and hurled himself at Terry.

'Get out,' choked Terry as he struggled with the two boys. 'Get out and leave us on our holiday. You're interrupting our holiday. It's Tess's holiday as well, you know. I won't let you spoil it.'

It took all of Imran and Mick's strength to hold him as Gallica managed to release Sharon.

At first Sharon was quite unable to stand up, and when she hauled herself to her feet she found she was unable to walk. Gallica half carried and half dragged her towards the door and through into the outer room.

Suddenly the room was full of policemen, hauling Terry off Mick, who reeled back bleeding, and Imran who, so far, had not been hurt. Then he saw Janata lying on the floor, with flames about to lick at his legs.

The next few minutes were total chaos, as Gallica dragged Sharon through the open window, the police fought with Terry, who proved as strong as he looked, and Mick and Imran tried to drag out Janata. His clothes were just starting to catch fire, and they beat at the flames fiercely with their bare hands. Janata was unconcious as they pulled him over the sill and, as they dumped him on the ground outside, Mick and Imran looked at their own hands. Mick's were worse; they were black and the pain in them was agonising. He staggered a few more paces and then sank to the ground as Imran bent over him.

Sharon sat with Gallica's arms around her as the fire sirens sounded over Starling Point and she saw the police dismantling the screen so that the fire engines could get as near to the blaze as possible. It was extraordinary when the screen came down for there was a vast audience standing there, and she felt as if she was part of a spectacle that had been specially designed for them. Then her attention was disrupted as the police carried a dazed but still feebly struggling Terry out of the smoke. They were all spluttering and coughing and they threw him face down on the ground while one of the policemen fitted handcuffs on his wrists. Then they moved him to one side to avoid the onrushing fire brigade with their hoses. Sharon limped towards Terry but Gallica put a restraining hand on her arm.

'I wouldn't go near him.'

'I want to see him.'

'But why?'

'Please.'

She let her go and Imran followed her over while the firemen trained their hoses through the window of the flat and an ambulance roared up for Mick and Janata. Imran didn't know what to do. He wanted to be with Mick and Janata but he also wanted to be with Sharon. He looked at her lovingly as she knelt beside Terry, who was coughing and choking with streaming eyes. He looked up from his trussed-up position as she bent over him.

'You OK?'

'They hit me,' he spluttered, but he looked all right. A police van moved in towards them and the police-men went to open the doors.

'Terry.'

'What?'

'I meant what I said.'

'What did you say?' He looked dazed and bemused.

124

'I said that I would come and see you wherever you go. And I will.'

He nodded and a slow smile broke over his features.

'Tess.'

'Yes, Terry?'

'Are you Tess?'

'No. But I'm a friend, Terry.'

'Where are they going to take me?'

'Somewhere to get you better.'

'Will they hurt me again?'

'I don't think they will again.'

'And you'll come and see me?'

'I want to. Do you want me to come?'

He nodded. Then he said, 'Did you have a good holiday, Tess?'

Sharon paused and then she said, 'I'll always remember it, Terry.'

Thirteen

Two weeks later Imran and Sharon took the train to the big mental hospital in Surrey where Terry had been taken. As they walked up the long, laurel-hedged drive she said: 'Thanks for coming with me.'

'I wanted to. How are Mick's hands now? I haven't seen him for a few days.'

'Much better. They've healed very quickly. He's practically OK again.'

'That was a brave thing he did.'

'You were both brave.'

'He's all right, is Mick.'

Sharon smiled. Mick and Imran were actually becoming good friends. 'I was surprised when he offered to help Janata move in tonight,' she said. 'We'll all have to start calling him Michael soon.'

Just outside the locked ward they met Terry's mother. She seemed very calm.

'How is he?' asked Sharon.

'Looking forward to seeing you.'

'I had a very difficult job convicing them that I should see him. But Imran's supported me all the way along the line.'

'So will I, my dear, and I'm hoping that his father will come round soon.'

'Do you think he will?'

'He might. You never know. Personally, I believe in miracles. But there's something I should ask you.'

'I think I know. You're frightened he'll begin to depend on me.'

'Something like that.'

'That's why I'm going with Imran. I want Terry to know where he stands. Has he mentioned Tess again?'

'I told him that I was sure he hadn't done her any harm and that the whole tragedy was just an accident. I've convinced myself of that too, now.' Her face was alight with a new hope. 'All I have to do is to get his dad to say the same thing and I don't think we'll hear her name again.'

'Has he been in any of his rages?'

'He's very quiet. Hardly says a thing. Do you want to go in now?'

Sharon steeled herself and Imran took her hand.

'We're ready,' he said.

One of the male nurses unlocked the door and took them into Terry's room. He was sitting in an armchair, looking out of the window.

'Hallo Terry,' she said.

Janata had quite recovered from the beating Terry had given him, although his face was still quite badly bruised, and he hadn't suffered any lasting effects from the fire. He lugged his bags out of the van that Mick had hired. His few possessions only half filled it, and as they carried them into the flat they had to pass the blackened and boarded-up site of the siege. There was no one about but Janata kept looking round so nervously that Mick stopped and plumped a table lamp and a couple of pictures down on the concrete walkway.

'What's up?' he asked with a grin.

'You know.'

'Don't worry, mate. It's not going to be easy, but you're at Starling Point and it's a mixture. Know what I mean?'

Janata looked at him doubtfully.

'Look. There are some right wallies living here, like my old man and a good few others. But we have to live with them. It's not easy for me or for you. But there are some decent people, too. Like my girlfriend Gallica. She's going to come and help us later. You got to remember one thing, Janata.'

'What's that?'

'You got mates and we're going to see you through.'